KNIGHTS

SOCCER

WRITTEN BY
RICARDO SANCHEZ

COVER AND INTERIOR ILLUSTRATED BY
IAN WARYANTO

COVER COLORS BY
OVERDRIVE STUDIO AT SPACE GOAT PRODUCTIONS

INTERIOR COLORS BY
KOMIKAKI STUDIO FEATURING SAW33 AT SPACE GOAT PRODUCTIONS

LETTERING BY
JAYMES REED

Sports Illustrated Kids Graphic Novels are published by
Stone Arch Books,
A Capstone Imprint
1710 Roe Crest Drive
North Mankato, Minnesota 56003
www.capstonepub.com

Text © 2015
Illustrations © 2015 Stone Arch Books

Cataloging-in-Publication Data is available on the
Library of Congress website.
ISBN: 978-1-4342-4165-8 (library binding)
ISBN: 978-1-4342-9182-0 (paperback)
ISBN: 978-1-4965-0092-2 (eBook)

Ashley C. Andersen Zantop PUBLISHER
Michael Dah EDITORIAL DIRECTOR
Sean Tulien EDITOR
Heather Kindseth CREATIVE DIRECTOR
Brann Garvey ART DIRECTOR
Hilary Wacholz DESIGNER

Summary: Steve's team is absolutely awesome in
practice. Everyone's talented and determined, and their
new quarterback, Aaron Corbin, throws bullets . . . so why
are the they struggling to win games? Steve notices
that Aaron seems to be afraid of getting hit. With a little
help from his teammates, Steve goes to great lengths to
toughen up Aaron only to discover that toughness isn't
the quarterback's actual problem.

Printed in the United States of America in
North Mankato, Minnesota
042018   000027

Sports Illustrated KIDS

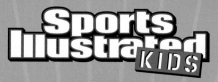

PRESENTS

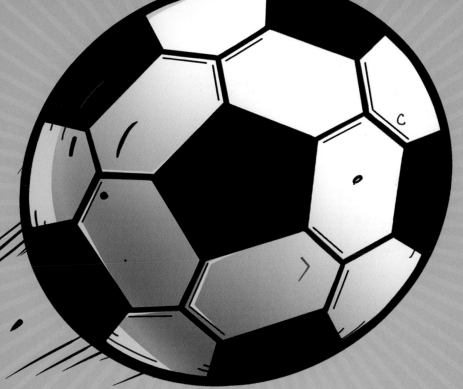

SPOTLIGHT SOCCER

STONE ARCH BOOKS

a Capstone Imprint

KNIGHTS LINEUP

FRANCO

HEIGHT: 5 feet, 6 inches

WEIGHT: 130 pounds

SKILLS: passing and daydreaming

MAX

HEIGHT: 5 feet, 2 inches

WEIGHT: 135 pounds

SKILLS: goaltending and making friends

KELLY

HEIGHT: 5 feet, 7 inches

WEIGHT: 155 pounds

SKILLS: shooting and flexing

MARTIN

HEIGHT: 5 feet, 1 inch

WEIGHT: 110 pounds

SKILLS: dribbling and ball-hogging

ISAIAH

HEIGHT: 5 feet, 5 inches

WEIGHT: 125 pounds

SKILLS: quick thinking and headers

ERIN

HEIGHT: 5 feet, 6 inches

WEIGHT: 125 pounds

SKILLS: cutting angles and getting open

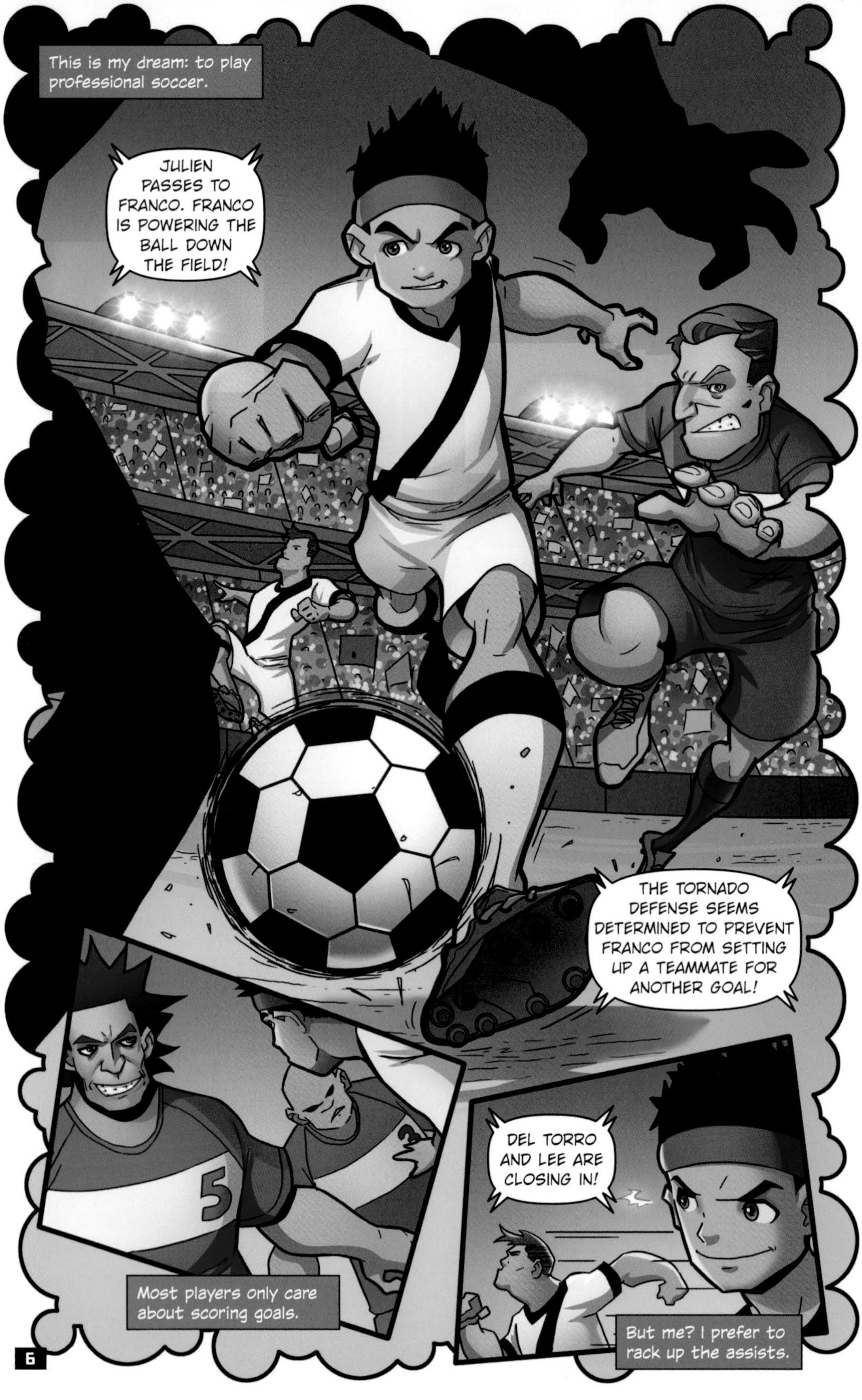
This is my dream: to play professional soccer.
JULIEN PASSES TO FRANCO. FRANCO IS POWERING THE BALL DOWN THE FIELD!
THE TORNADO DEFENSE SEEMS DETERMINED TO PREVENT FRANCO FROM SETTING UP A TEAMMATE FOR ANOTHER GOAL!
5
Most players only care about scoring goals.
DEL TORRO AND LEE ARE CLOSING IN!
But me? I prefer to rack up the assists.

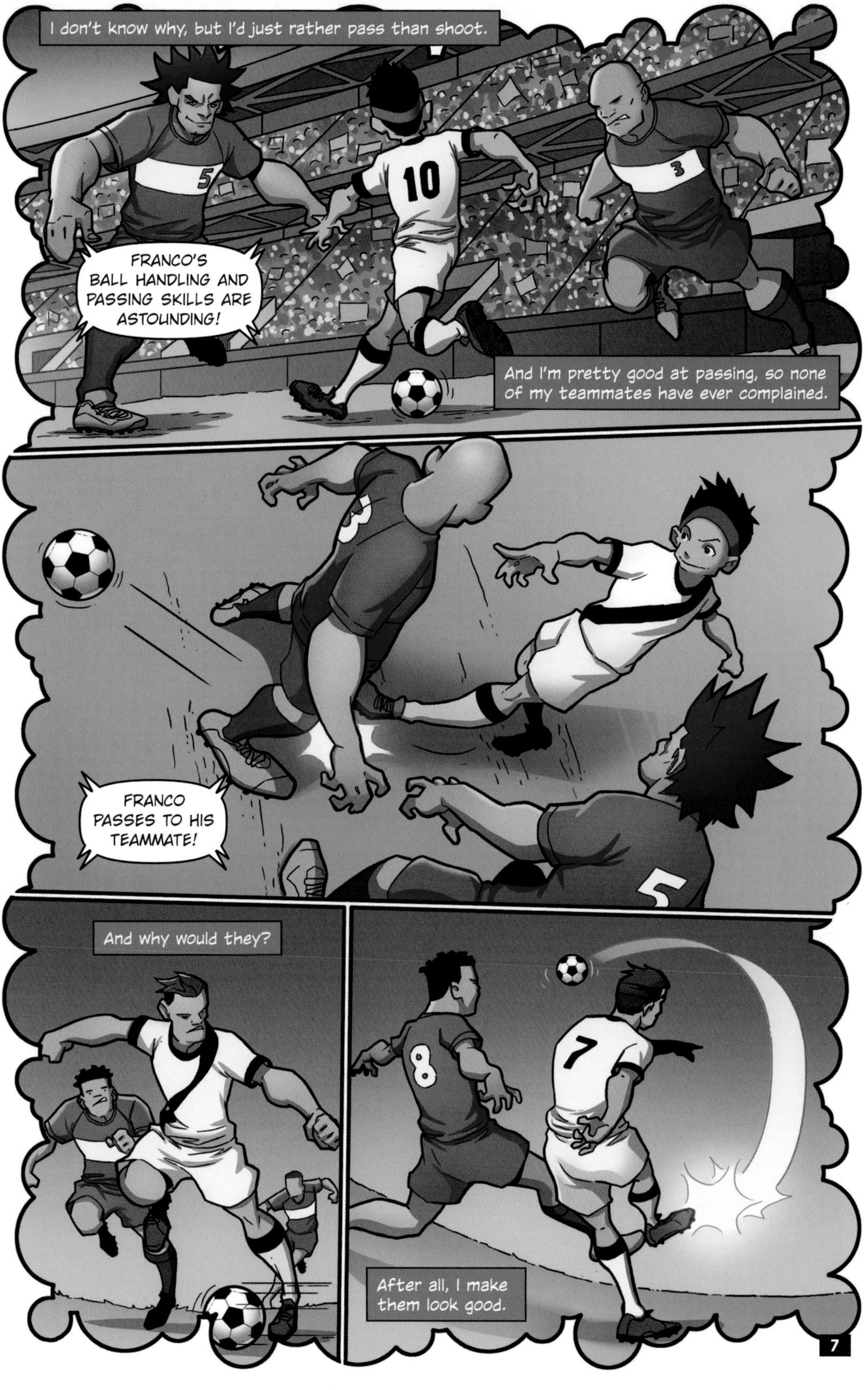
I don't know why, but I'd just rather pass than shoot.
FRANCO'S BALL HANDLING AND PASSING SKILLS ARE ASTOUNDING!
And I'm pretty good at passing, so none of my teammates have ever complained.
FRANCO PASSES TO HIS TEAMMATE!
And why would they?
After all, I make them look good.

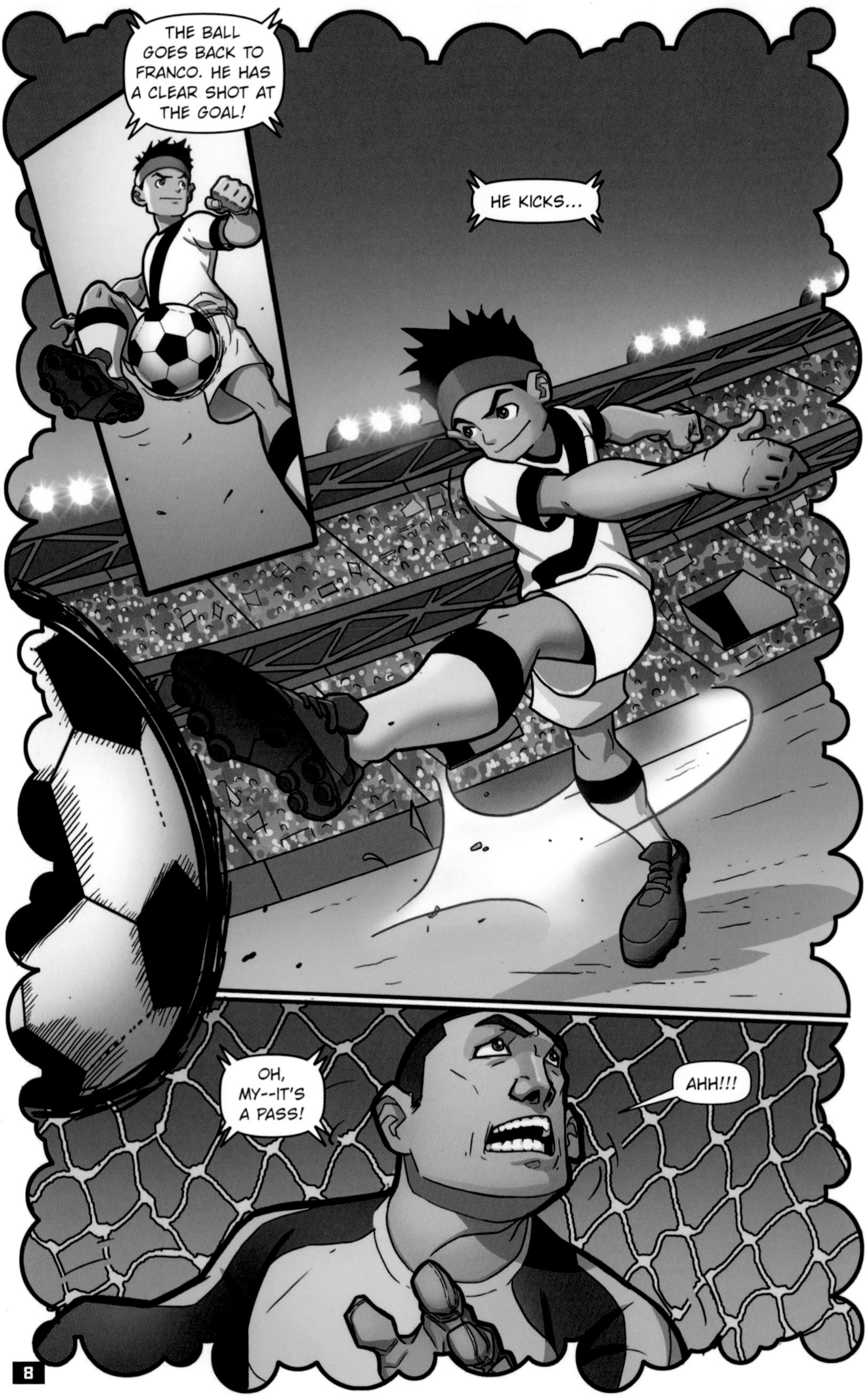
THE BALL GOES BACK TO FRANCO. HE HAS A CLEAR SHOT AT THE GOAL!
HE KICKS...
OH, MY--IT'S A PASS!
AHH!!!

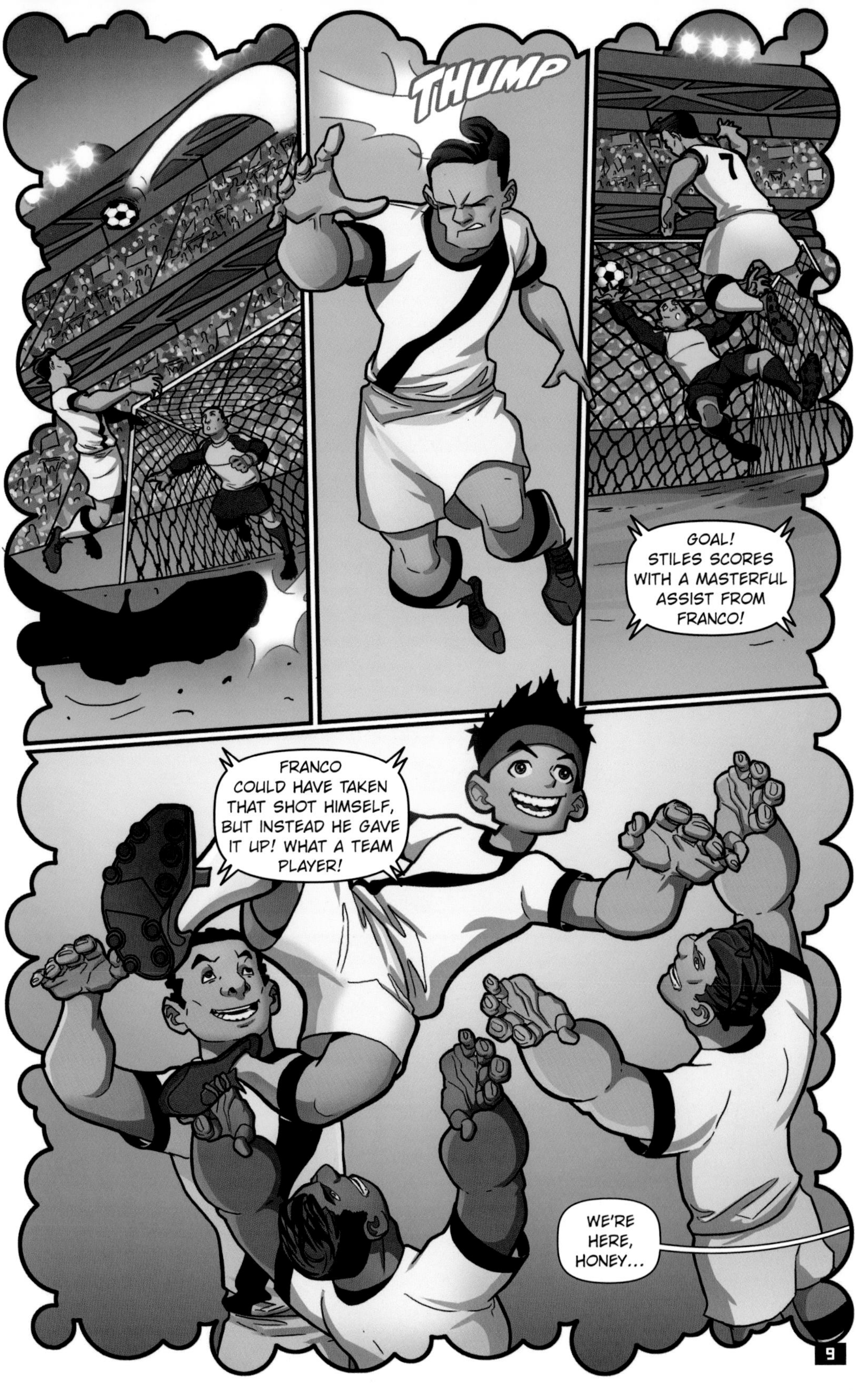
THUMP
GOAL! STILES SCORES WITH A MASTERFUL ASSIST FROM FRANCO!
FRANCO COULD HAVE TAKEN THAT SHOT HIMSELF, BUT INSTEAD HE GAVE IT UP! WHAT A TEAM PLAYER!
WE'RE HERE, HONEY...

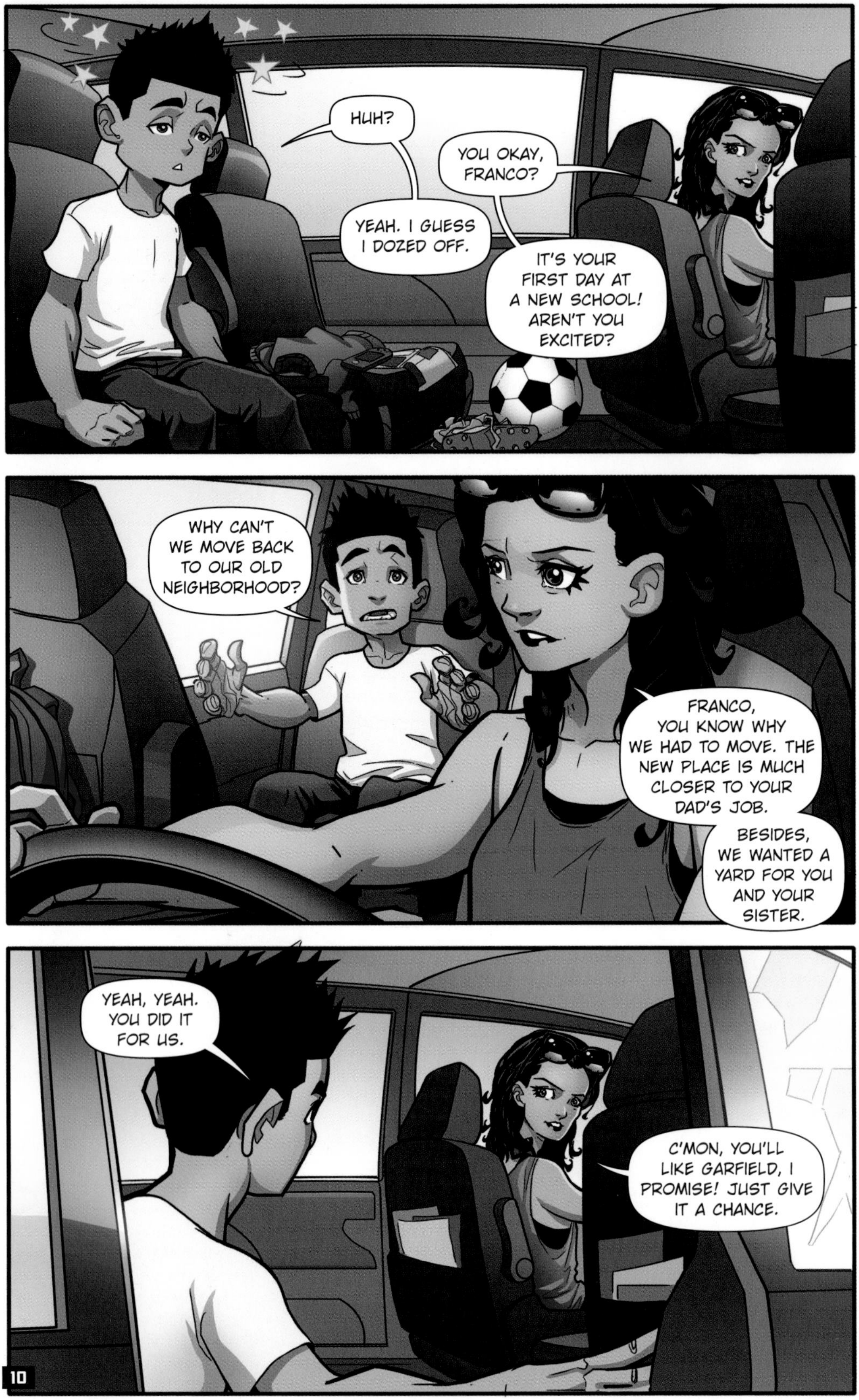
HUH?
YOU OKAY, FRANCO?
YEAH. I GUESS I DOZED OFF.
IT'S YOUR FIRST DAY AT A NEW SCHOOL! AREN'T YOU EXCITED?
WHY CAN'T WE MOVE BACK TO OUR OLD NEIGHBORHOOD?
FRANCO, YOU KNOW WHY WE HAD TO MOVE. THE NEW PLACE IS MUCH CLOSER TO YOUR DAD'S JOB.
BESIDES, WE WANTED A YARD FOR YOU AND YOUR SISTER.
YEAH, YEAH. YOU DID IT FOR US.
C'MON, YOU'LL LIKE GARFIELD, I PROMISE! JUST GIVE IT A CHANCE.

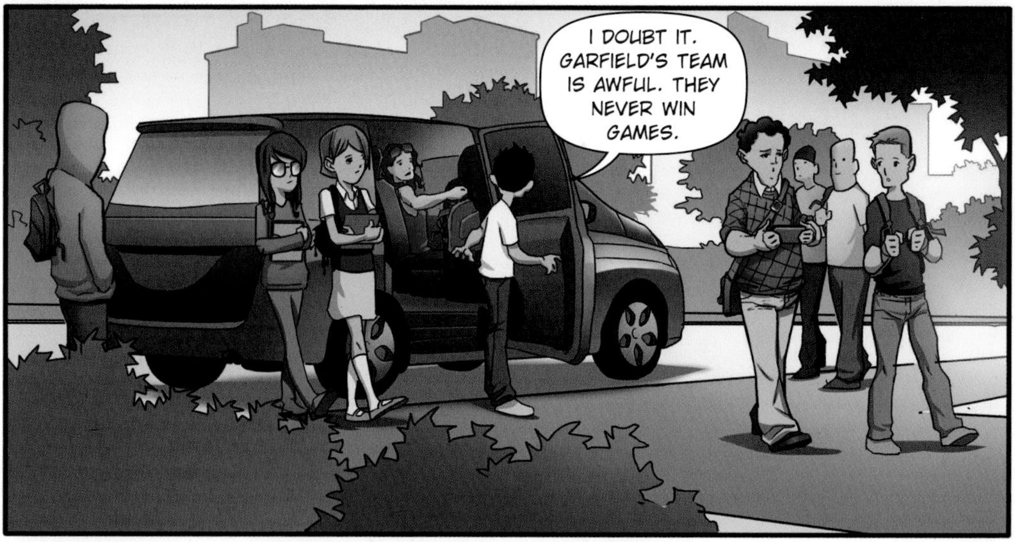
I DOUBT IT. GARFIELD'S TEAM IS AWFUL. THEY NEVER WIN GAMES.

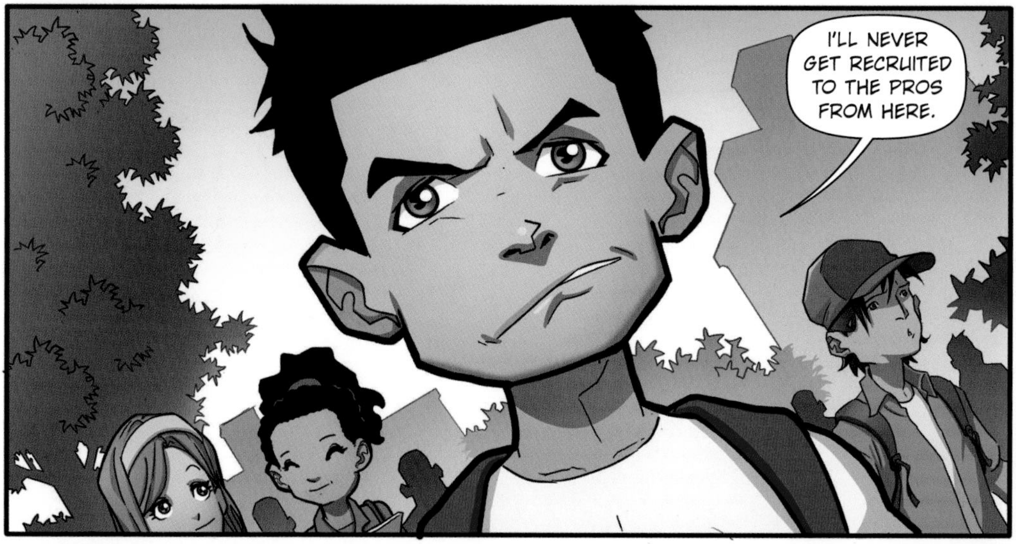
I'LL NEVER GET RECRUITED TO THE PROS FROM HERE.

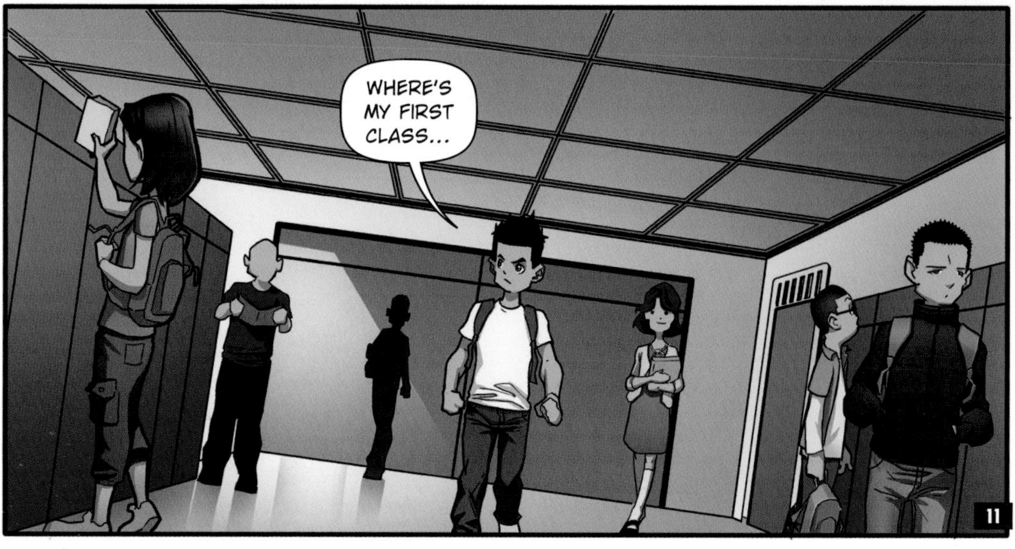
WHERE'S MY FIRST CLASS...

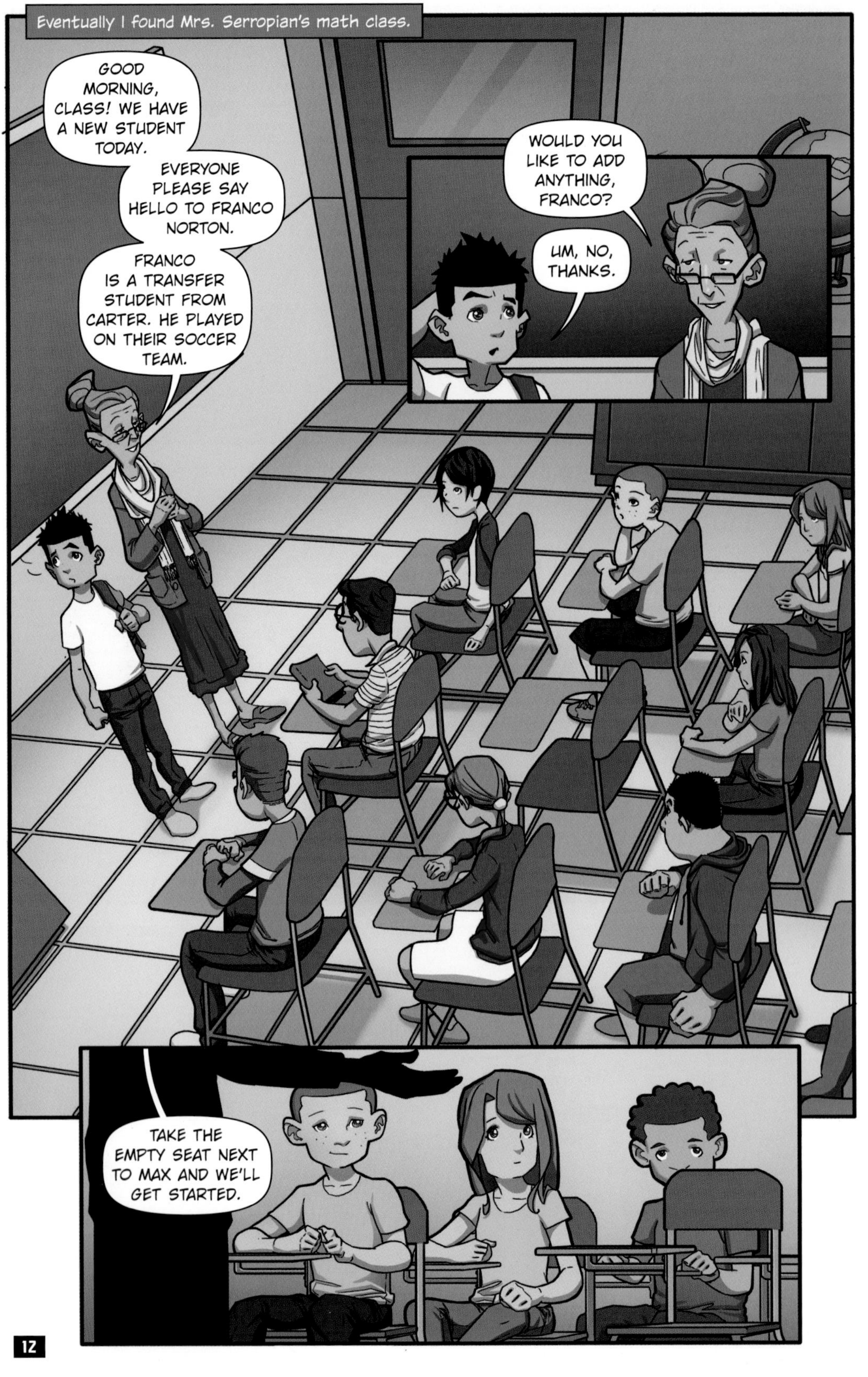
Eventually I found Mrs. Serropian's math class.
GOOD MORNING, CLASS! WE HAVE A NEW STUDENT TODAY.
EVERYONE PLEASE SAY HELLO TO FRANCO NORTON.
FRANCO IS A TRANSFER STUDENT FROM CARTER. HE PLAYED ON THEIR SOCCER TEAM.
WOULD YOU LIKE TO ADD ANYTHING, FRANCO?
UM, NO, THANKS.
TAKE THE EMPTY SEAT NEXT TO MAX AND WE'LL GET STARTED.

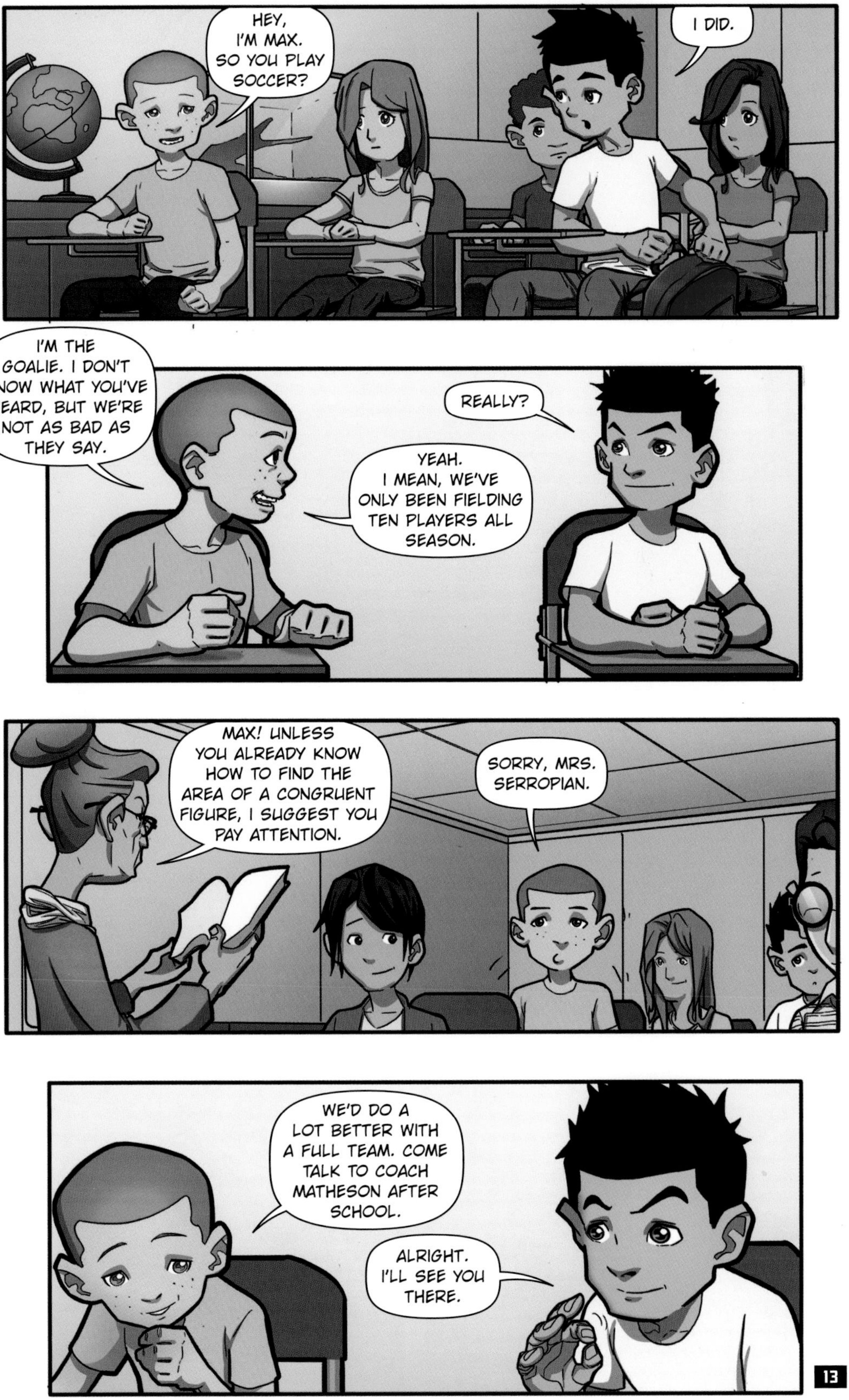
HEY, I'M MAX. SO YOU PLAY SOCCER?
I DID.
I'M THE GOALIE. I DON'T KNOW WHAT YOU'VE HEARD, BUT WE'RE NOT AS BAD AS THEY SAY.
REALLY?
YEAH. I MEAN, WE'VE ONLY BEEN FIELDING TEN PLAYERS ALL SEASON.
MAX! UNLESS YOU ALREADY KNOW HOW TO FIND THE AREA OF A CONGRUENT FIGURE, I SUGGEST YOU PAY ATTENTION.
SORRY, MRS. SERROPIAN.
WE'D DO A LOT BETTER WITH A FULL TEAM. COME TALK TO COACH MATHESON AFTER SCHOOL.
ALRIGHT. I'LL SEE YOU THERE.

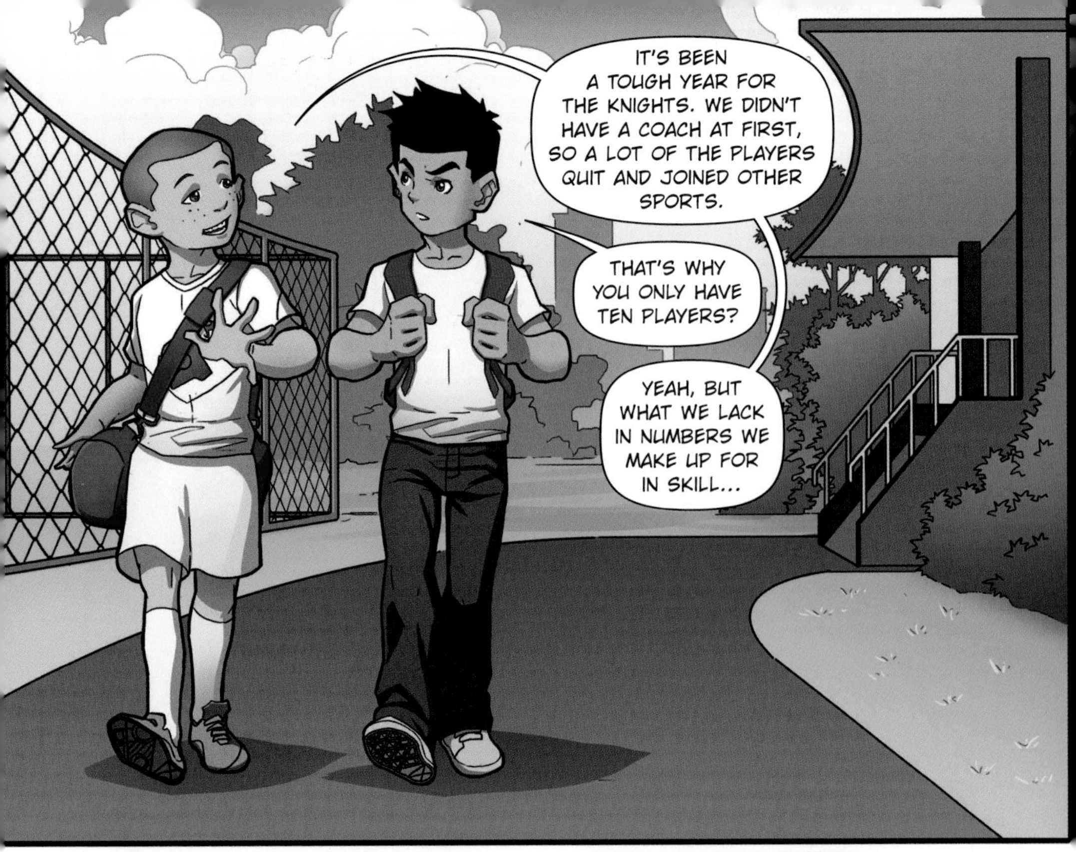
IT'S BEEN A TOUGH YEAR FOR THE KNIGHTS. WE DIDN'T HAVE A COACH AT FIRST, SO A LOT OF THE PLAYERS QUIT AND JOINED OTHER SPORTS.
THAT'S WHY YOU ONLY HAVE TEN PLAYERS?
YEAH, BUT WHAT WE LACK IN NUMBERS WE MAKE UP FOR IN SKILL...

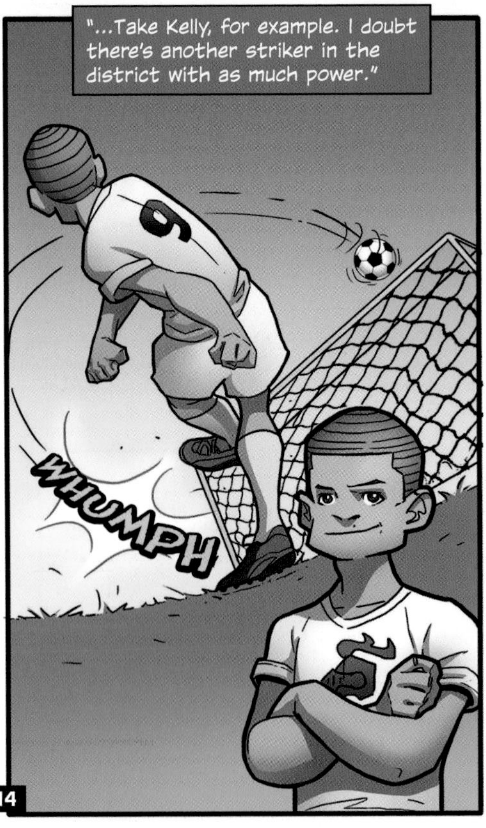
"...Take Kelly, for example. I doubt there's another striker in the district with as much power."
WHUMPH

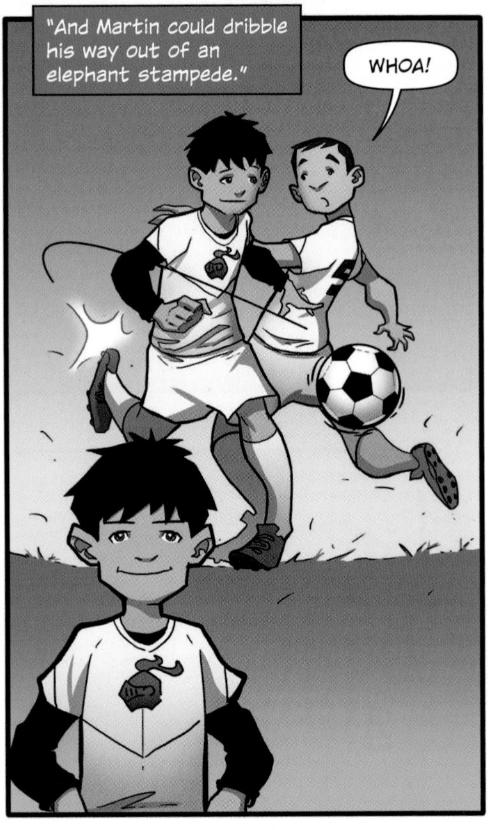
"And Martin could dribble his way out of an elephant stampede."
WHOA!

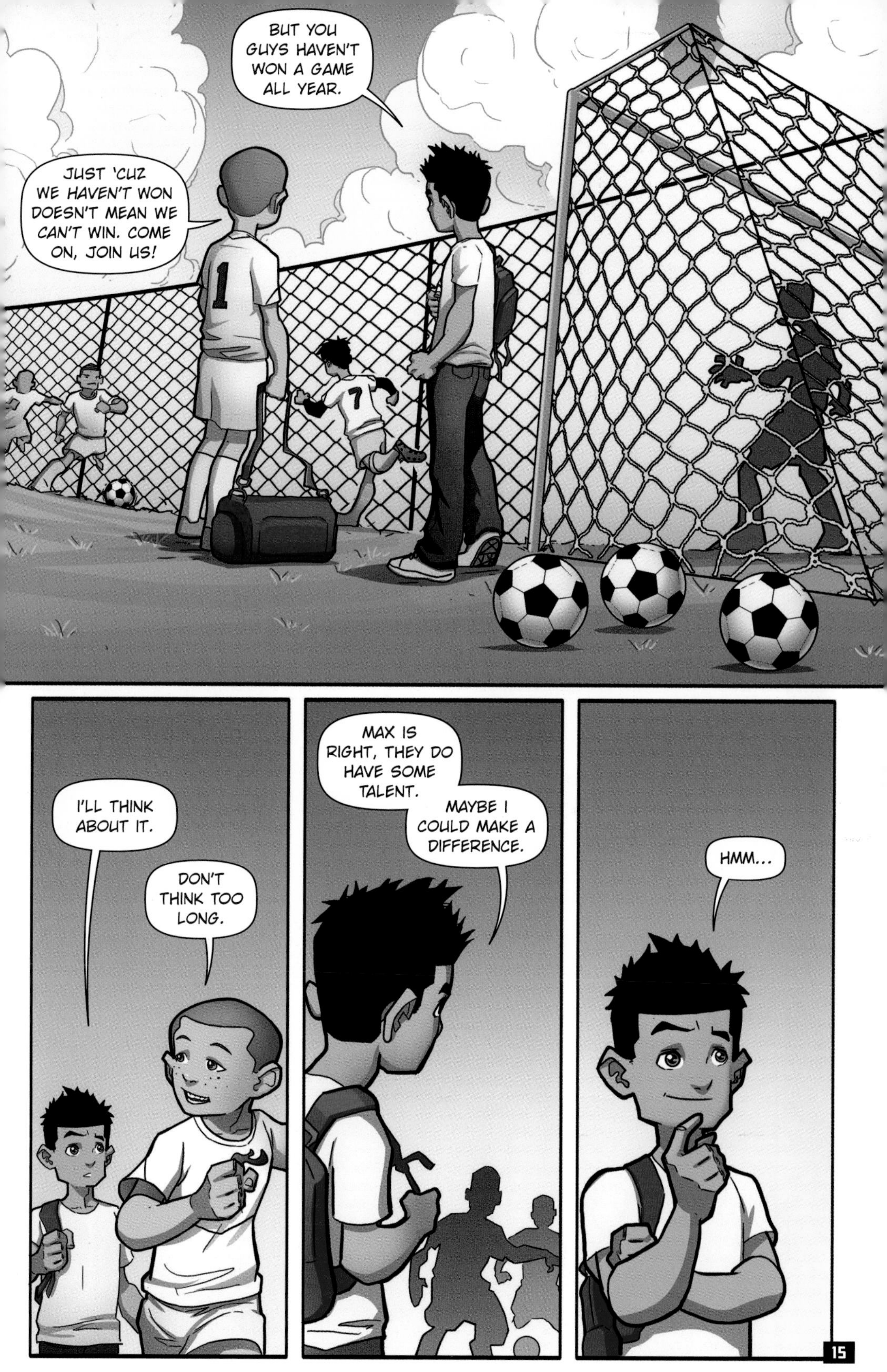
BUT YOU GUYS HAVEN'T WON A GAME ALL YEAR.
JUST 'CUZ WE HAVEN'T WON DOESN'T MEAN WE CAN'T WIN. COME ON, JOIN US!
I'LL THINK ABOUT IT.
DON'T THINK TOO LONG.
MAX IS RIGHT, THEY DO HAVE SOME TALENT.
MAYBE I COULD MAKE A DIFFERENCE.
HMM...

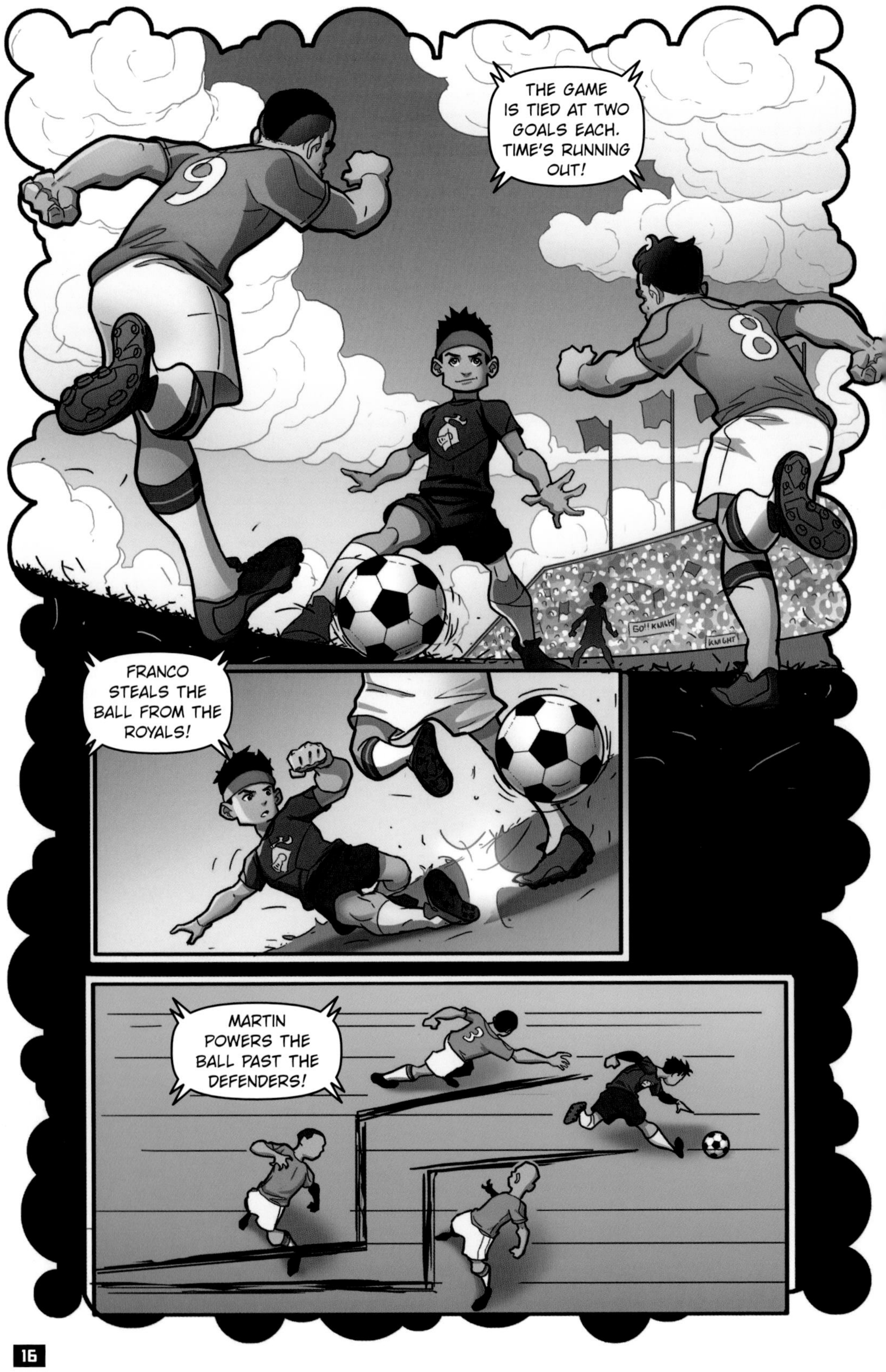
THE GAME IS TIED AT TWO GOALS EACH. TIME'S RUNNING OUT!
FRANCO STEALS THE BALL FROM THE ROYALS!
MARTIN POWERS THE BALL PAST THE DEFENDERS!

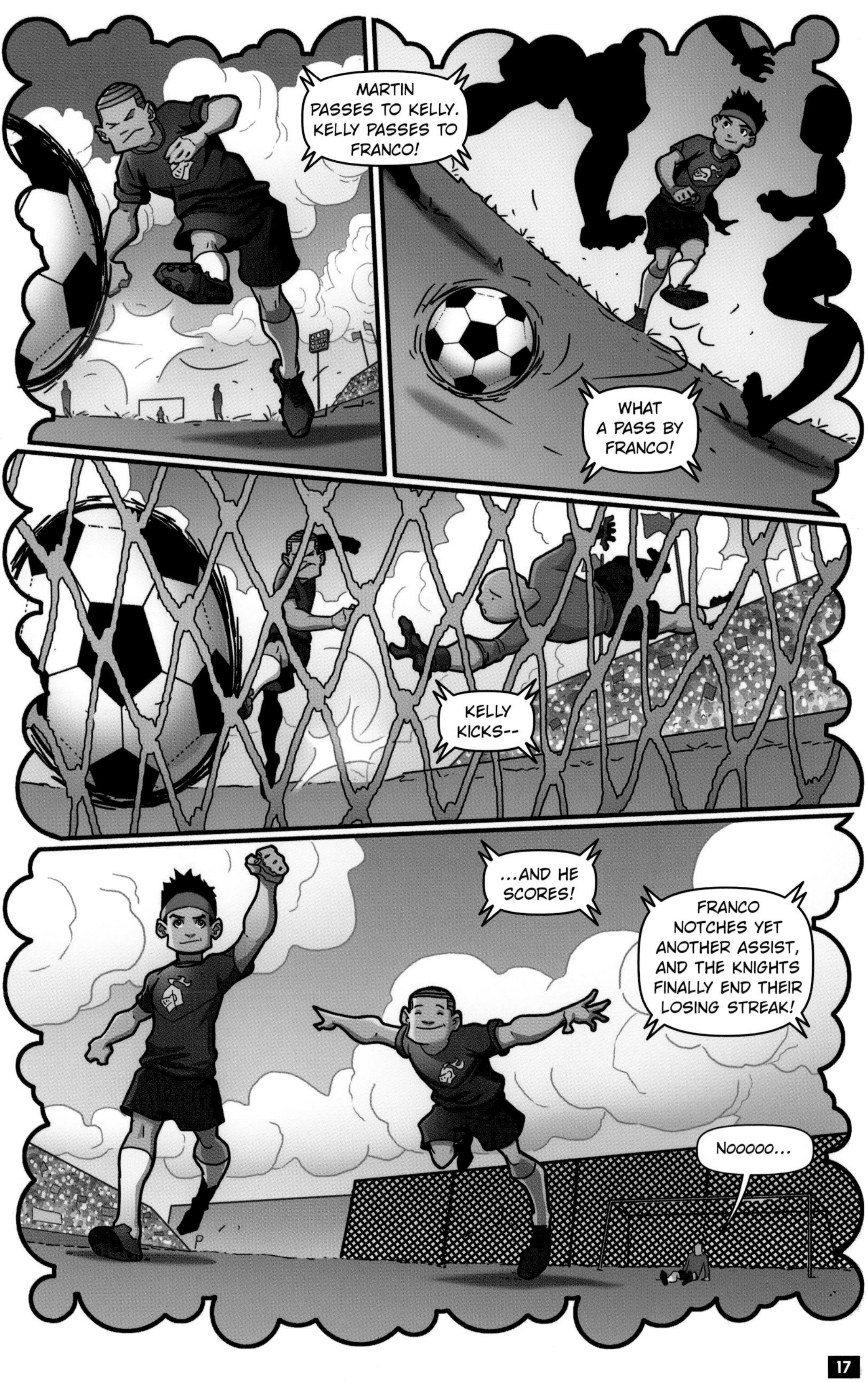

MARTIN PASSES TO KELLY. KELLY PASSES TO FRANCO!
WHAT A PASS BY FRANCO!
KELLY KICKS--
...AND HE SCORES!
FRANCO NOTCHES YET ANOTHER ASSIST, AND THE KNIGHTS FINALLY END THEIR LOSING STREAK!
Nooooo...

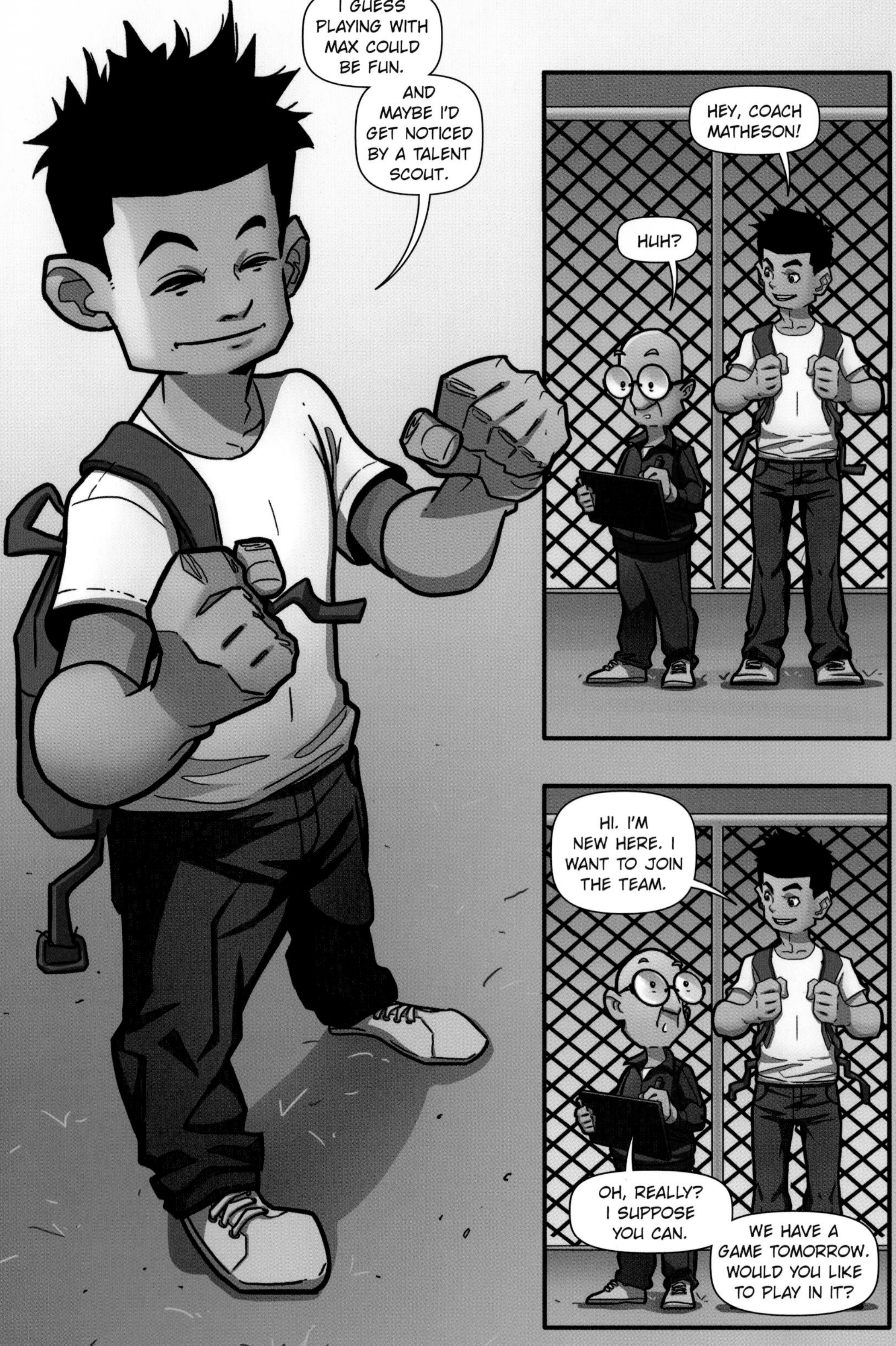
I GUESS PLAYING WITH MAX COULD BE FUN.
AND MAYBE I'D GET NOTICED BY A TALENT SCOUT.
HEY, COACH MATHESON!
HUH?
HI. I'M NEW HERE. I WANT TO JOIN THE TEAM.
OH, REALLY? I SUPPOSE YOU CAN.
WE HAVE A GAME TOMORROW. WOULD YOU LIKE TO PLAY IN IT?

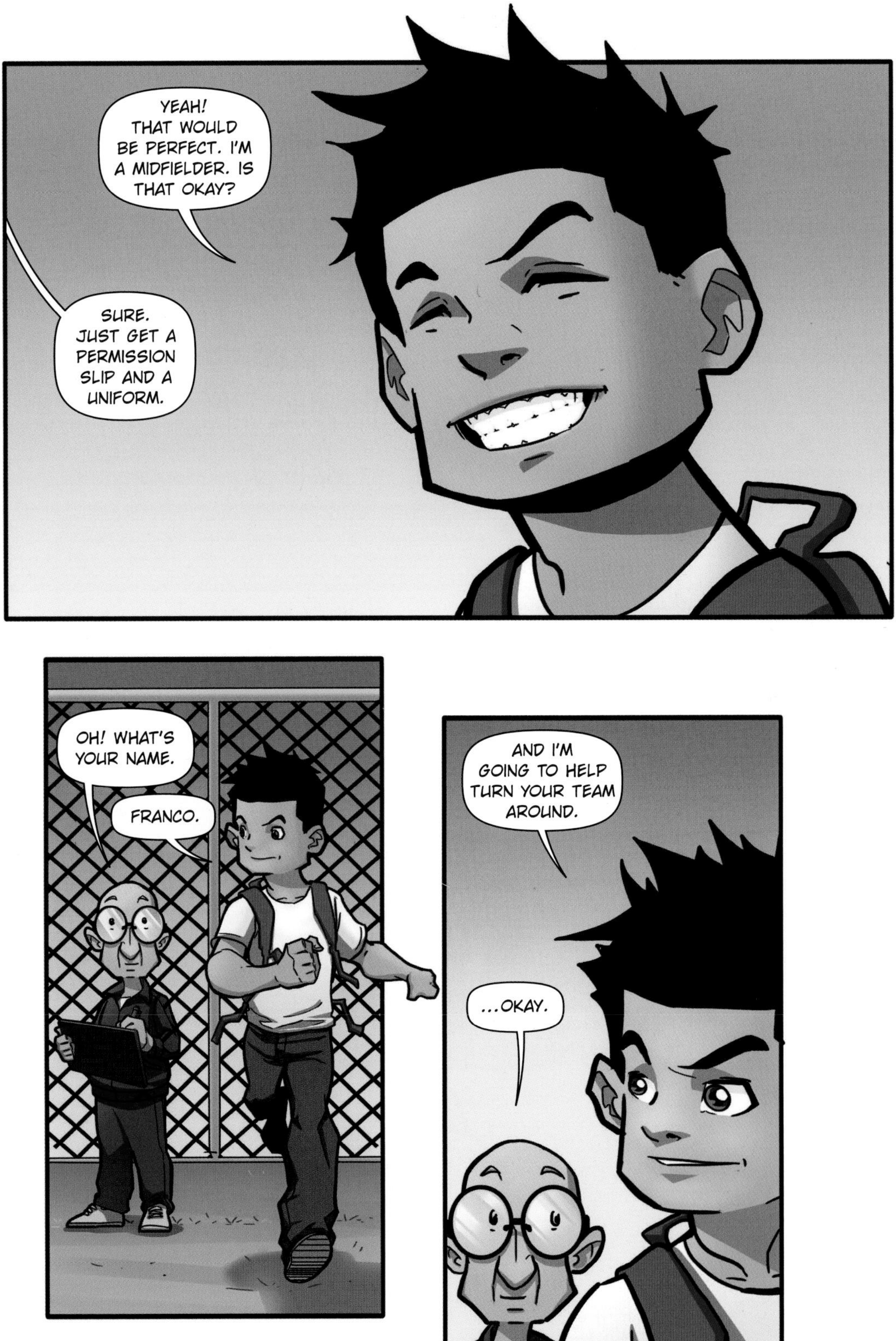
YEAH! THAT WOULD BE PERFECT. I'M A MIDFIELDER. IS THAT OKAY?
SURE. JUST GET A PERMISSION SLIP AND A UNIFORM.
OH! WHAT'S YOUR NAME.
FRANCO.
AND I'M GOING TO HELP TURN YOUR TEAM AROUND.
...OKAY.

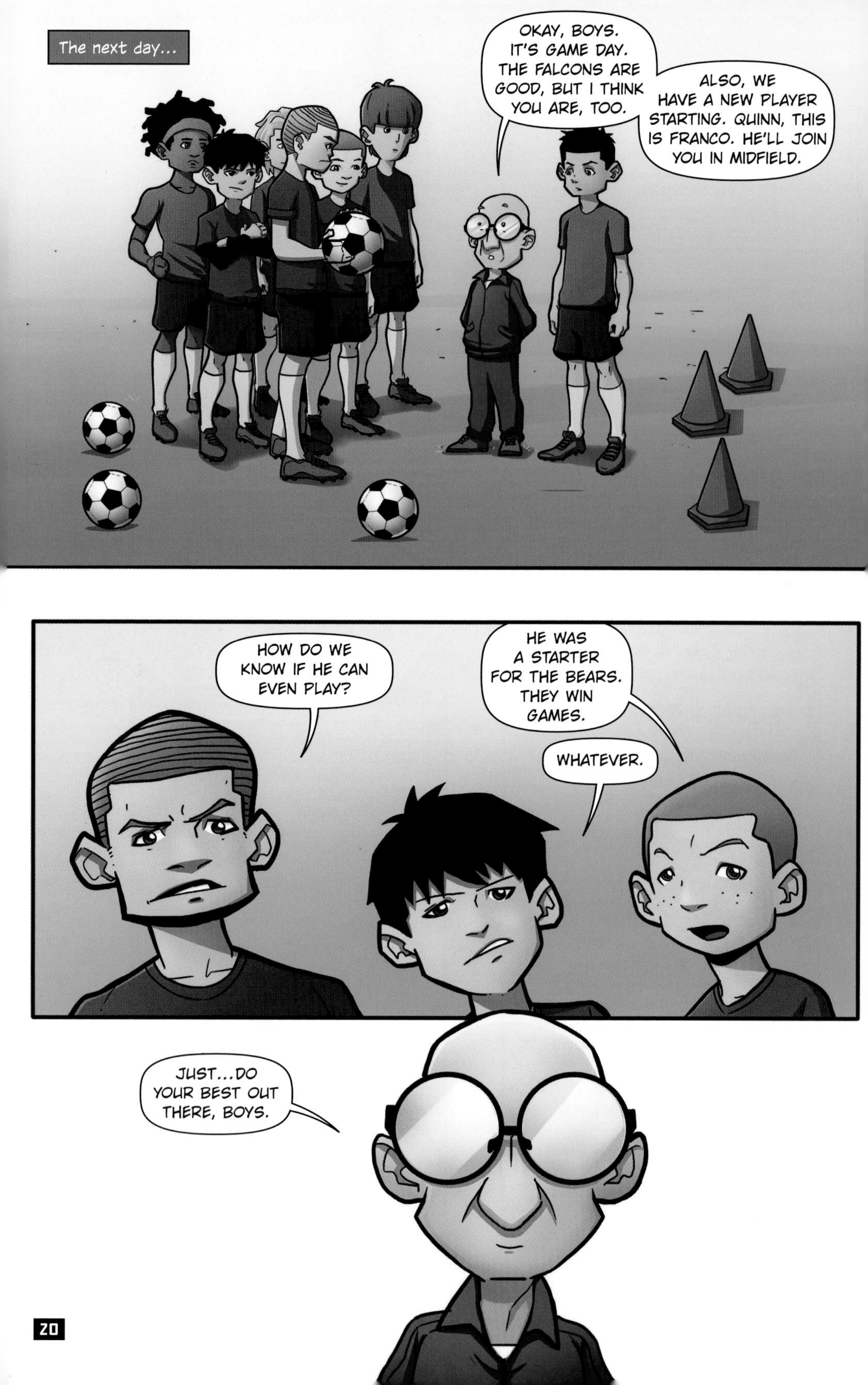
The next day...
OKAY, BOYS. IT'S GAME DAY. THE FALCONS ARE GOOD, BUT I THINK YOU ARE, TOO.
ALSO, WE HAVE A NEW PLAYER STARTING. QUINN, THIS IS FRANCO. HE'LL JOIN YOU IN MIDFIELD.
HOW DO WE KNOW IF HE CAN EVEN PLAY?
HE WAS A STARTER FOR THE BEARS. THEY WIN GAMES.
WHATEVER.
JUST...DO YOUR BEST OUT THERE, BOYS.

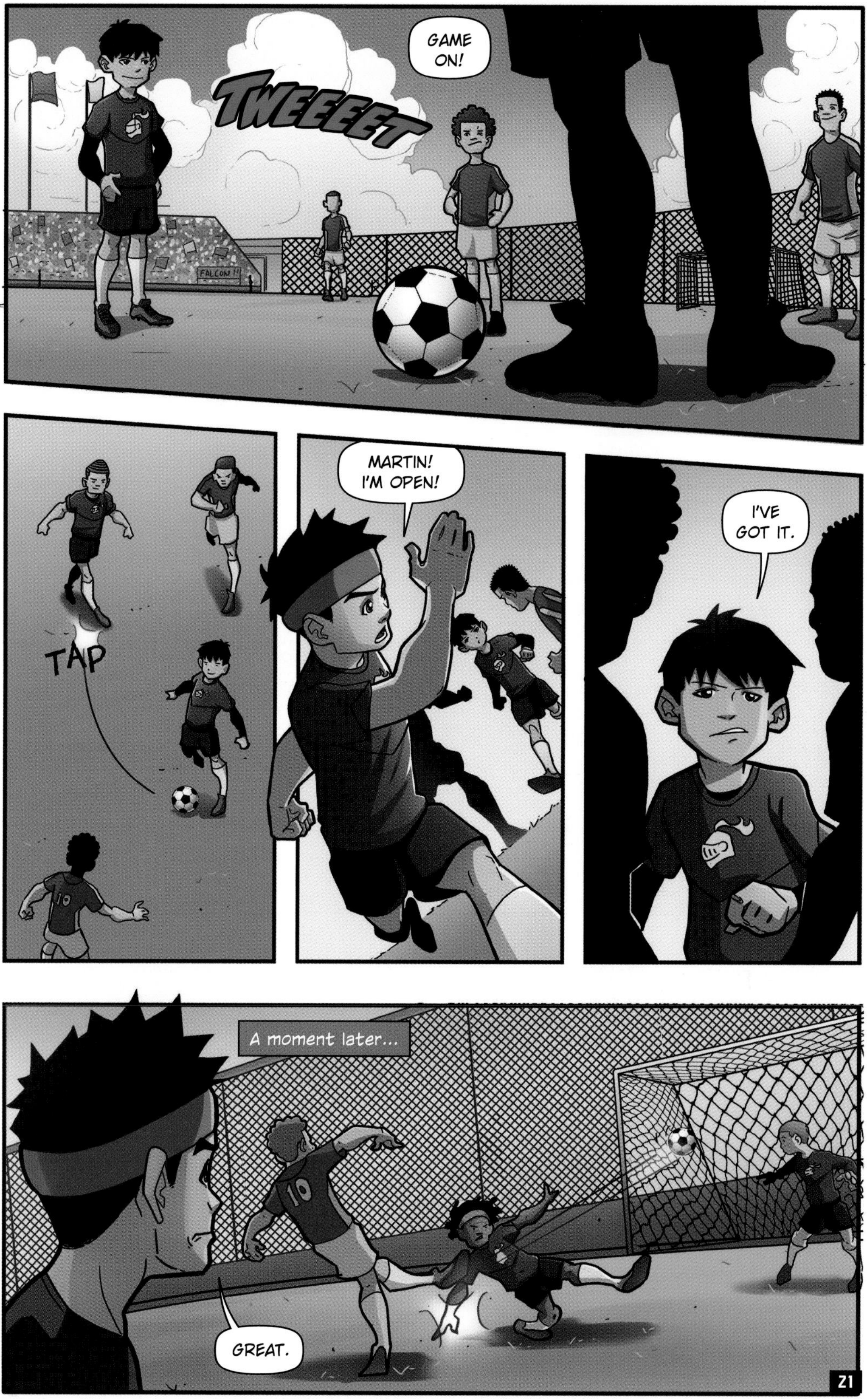

GAME ON!
TWEEEEET
FALCON!!
TAP
MARTIN! I'M OPEN!
I'VE GOT IT.
A moment later...
GREAT.

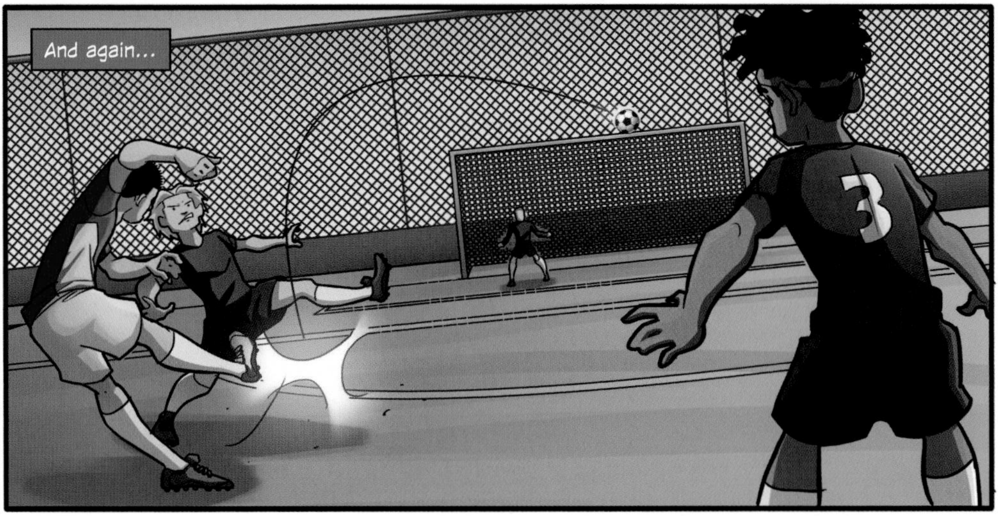
And again...

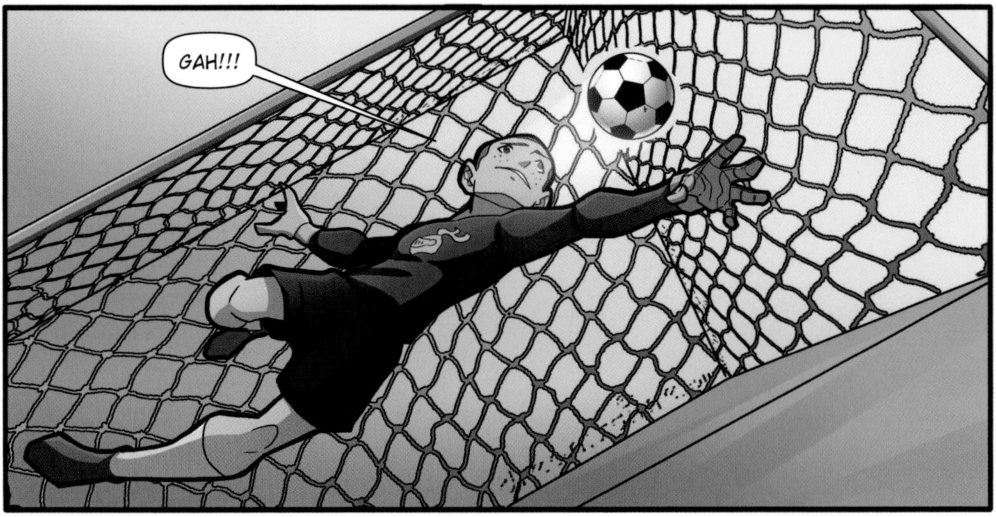
GAH!!!

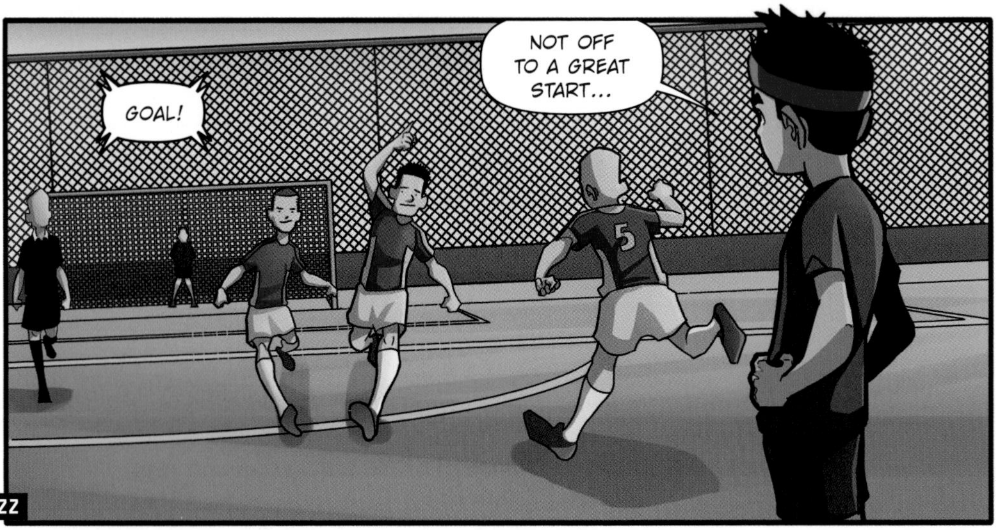
GOAL!
NOT OFF TO A GREAT START...

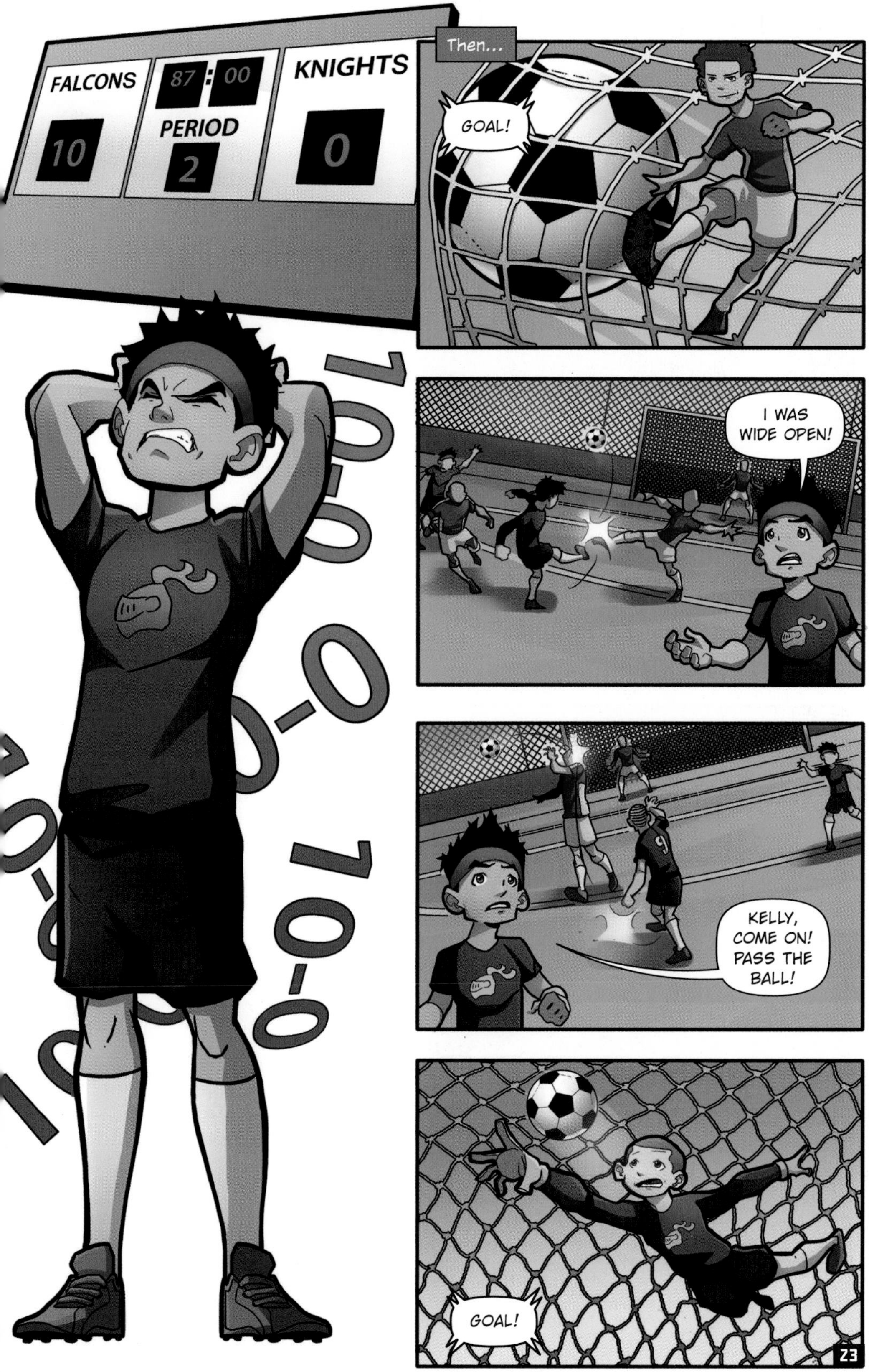

FALCONS
87 : 00
KNIGHTS
10
PERIOD
2
0
Then...
GOAL!
I WAS WIDE OPEN!
KELLY, COME ON! PASS THE BALL!
GOAL!

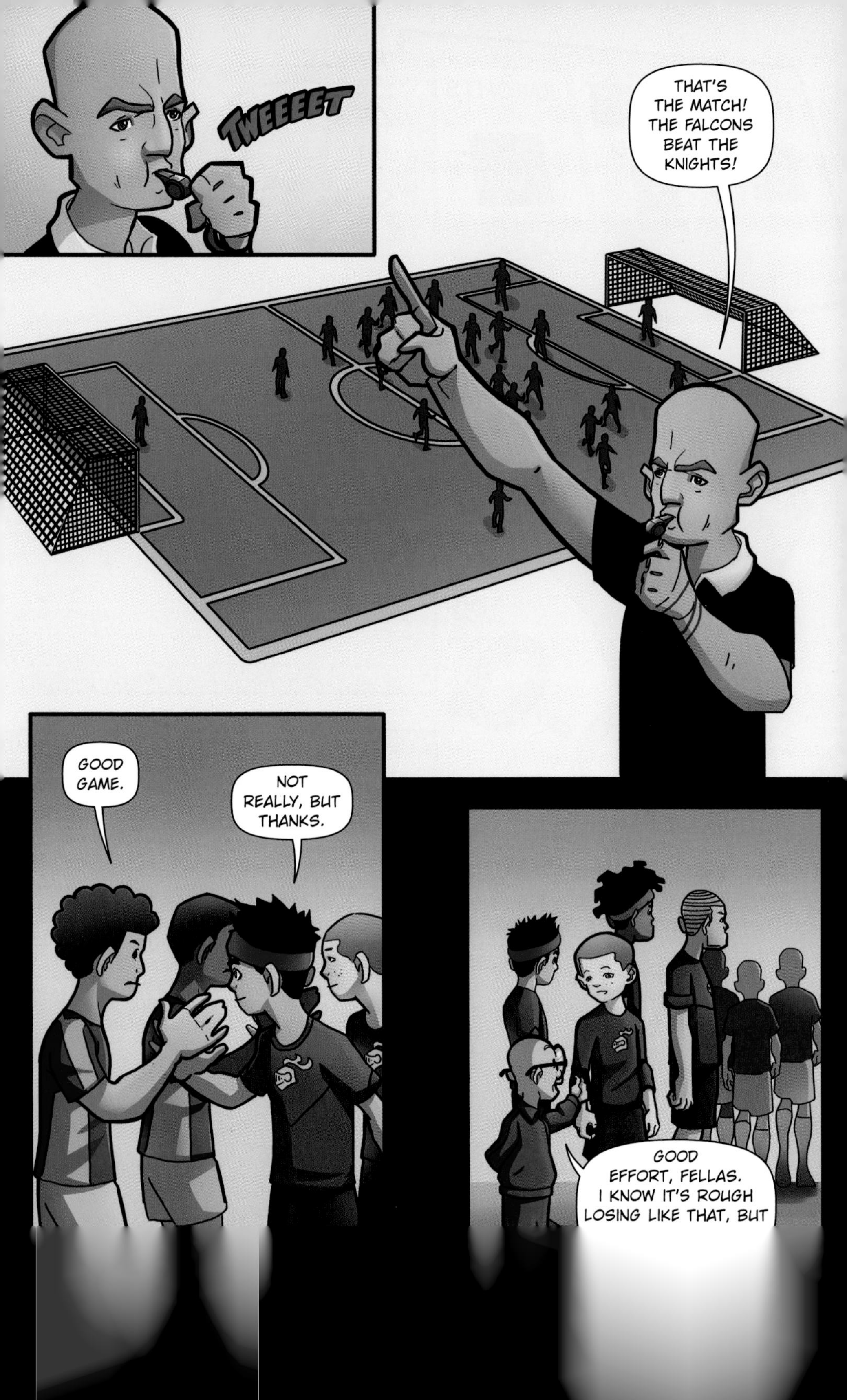
TWEEEEET
THAT'S THE MATCH! THE FALCONS BEAT THE KNIGHTS!
GOOD GAME.
NOT REALLY, BUT THANKS.
GOOD EFFORT, FELLAS. I KNOW IT'S ROUGH LOSING LIKE THAT, BUT

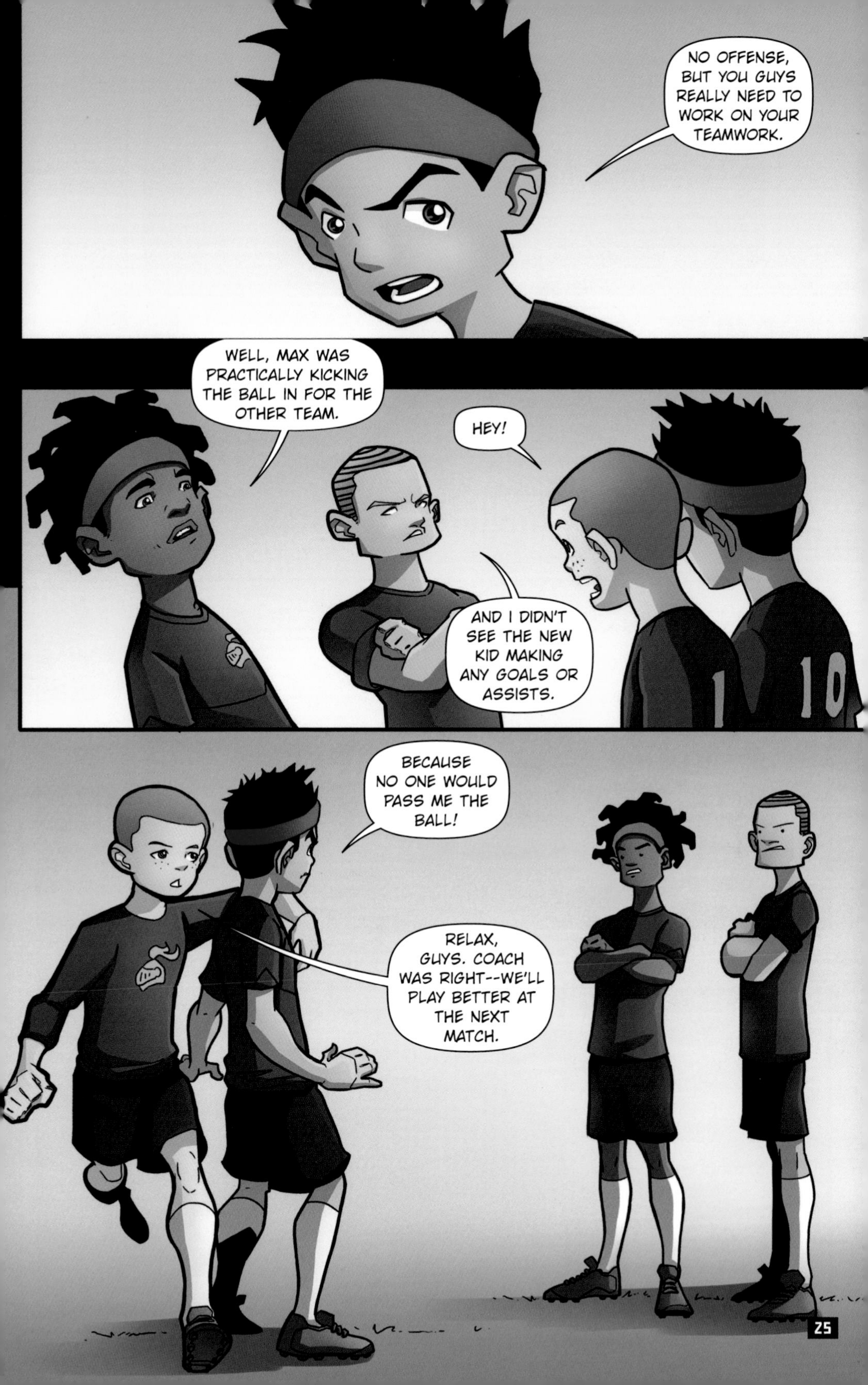
NO OFFENSE, BUT YOU GUYS REALLY NEED TO WORK ON YOUR TEAMWORK.
WELL, MAX WAS PRACTICALLY KICKING THE BALL IN FOR THE OTHER TEAM.
HEY!
AND I DIDN'T SEE THE NEW KID MAKING ANY GOALS OR ASSISTS.
BECAUSE NO ONE WOULD PASS ME THE BALL!
RELAX, GUYS. COACH WAS RIGHT--WE'LL PLAY BETTER AT THE NEXT MATCH.

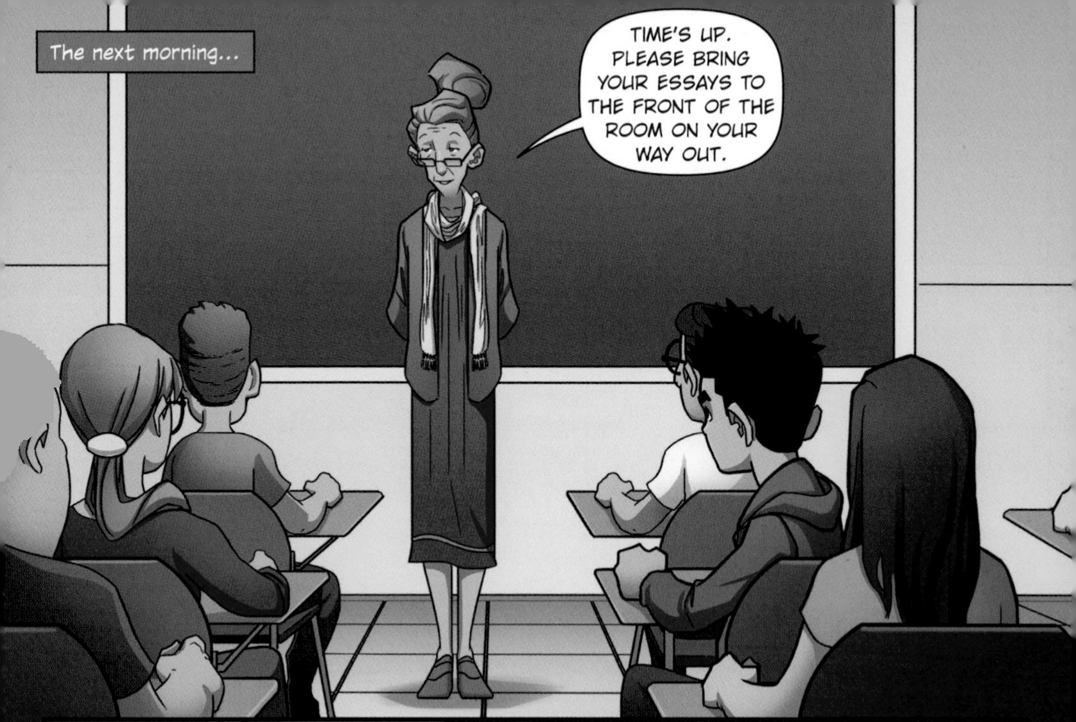
The next morning...
TIME'S UP. PLEASE BRING YOUR ESSAYS TO THE FRONT OF THE ROOM ON YOUR WAY OUT.

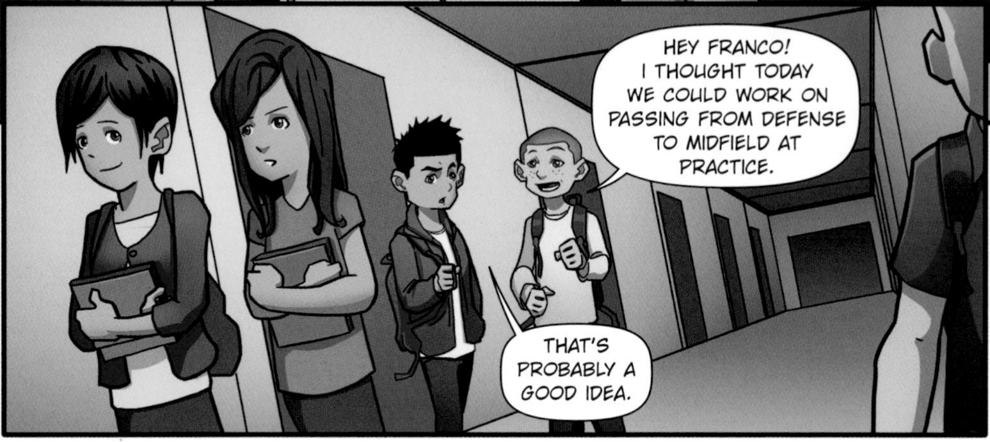
HEY FRANCO! I THOUGHT TODAY WE COULD WORK ON PASSING FROM DEFENSE TO MIDFIELD AT PRACTICE.
THAT'S PROBABLY A GOOD IDEA.

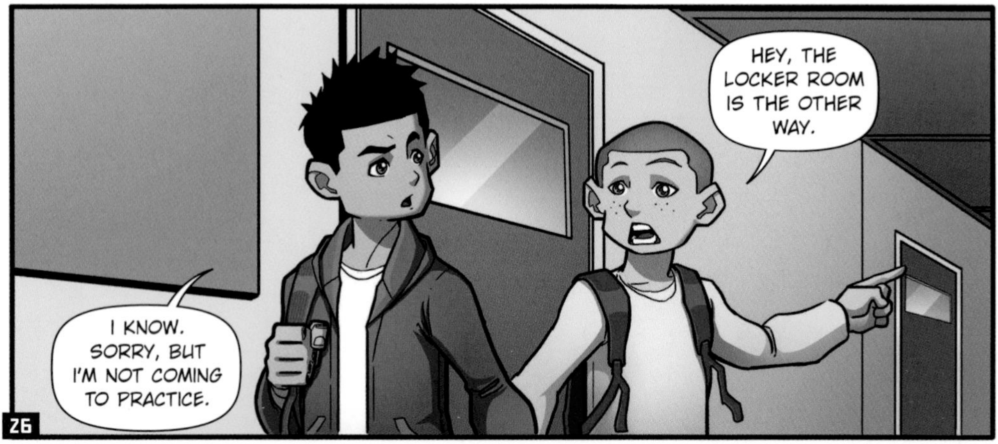
HEY, THE LOCKER ROOM IS THE OTHER WAY.
I KNOW. SORRY, BUT I'M NOT COMING TO PRACTICE.

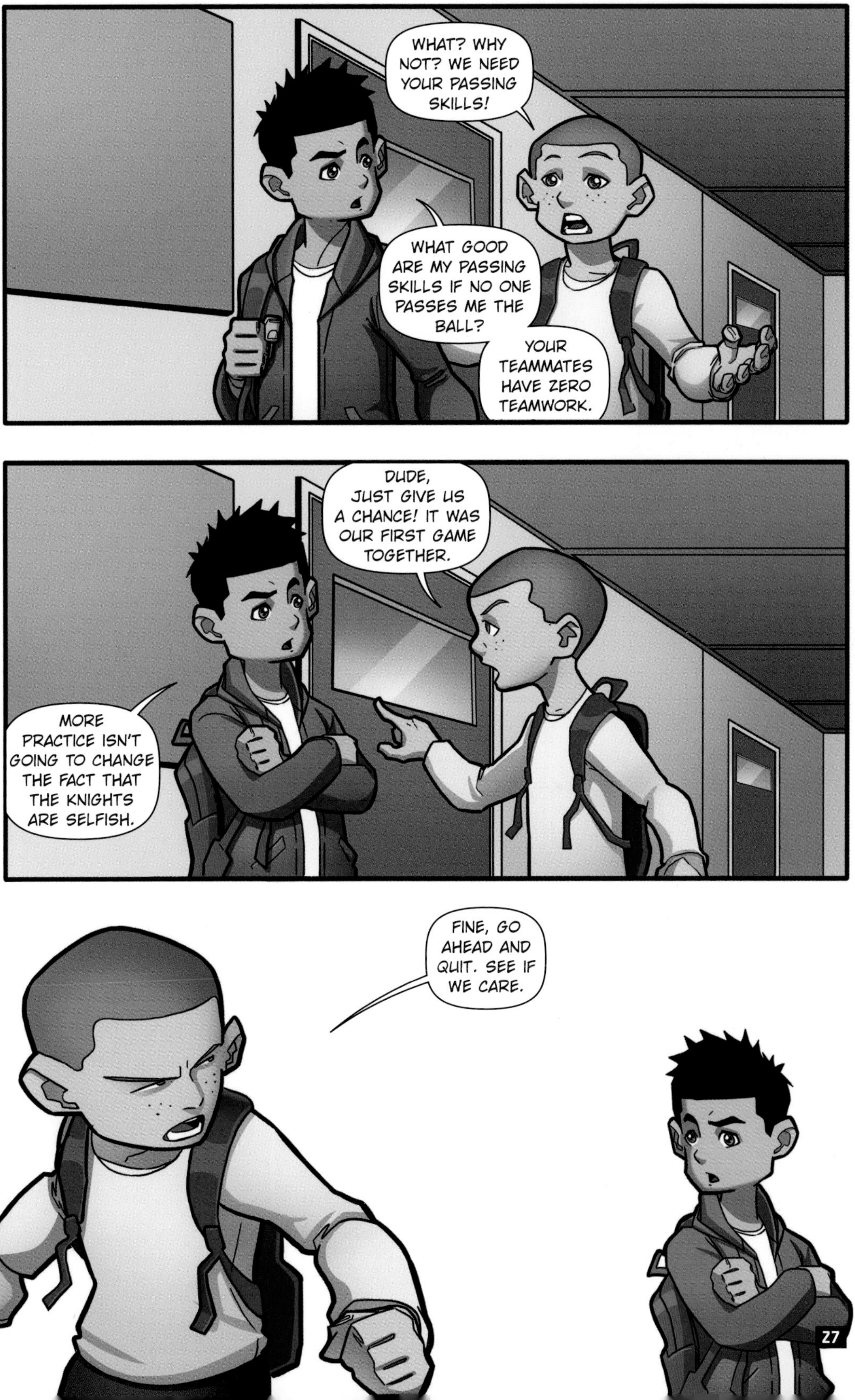
WHAT? WHY NOT? WE NEED YOUR PASSING SKILLS!
WHAT GOOD ARE MY PASSING SKILLS IF NO ONE PASSES ME THE BALL?
YOUR TEAMMATES HAVE ZERO TEAMWORK.
DUDE, JUST GIVE US A CHANCE! IT WAS OUR FIRST GAME TOGETHER.
MORE PRACTICE ISN'T GOING TO CHANGE THE FACT THAT THE KNIGHTS ARE SELFISH.
FINE, GO AHEAD AND QUIT. SEE IF WE CARE.

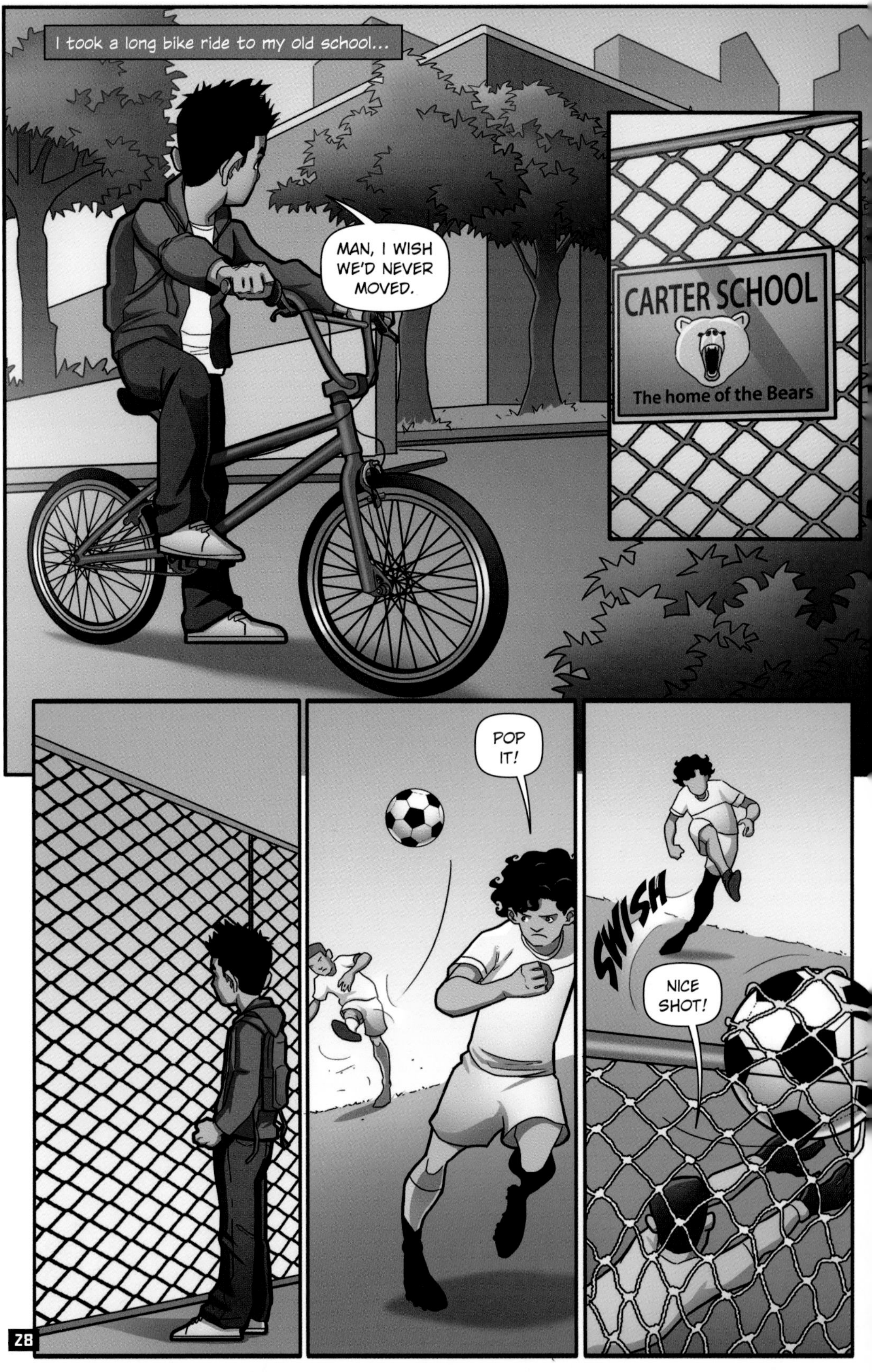
I took a long bike ride to my old school...
MAN, I WISH WE'D NEVER MOVED.
CARTER SCHOOL
The home of the Bears
POP IT!
SWISH
NICE SHOT!

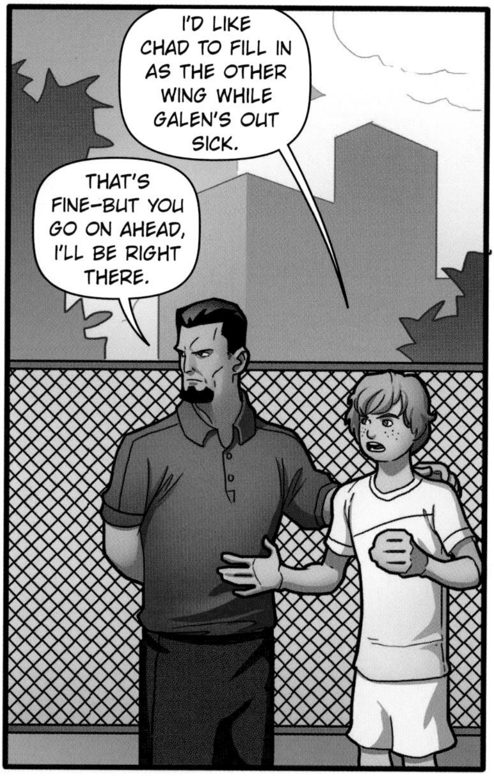
I'D LIKE CHAD TO FILL IN AS THE OTHER WING WHILE GALEN'S OUT SICK.
THAT'S FINE—BUT YOU GO ON AHEAD, I'LL BE RIGHT THERE.

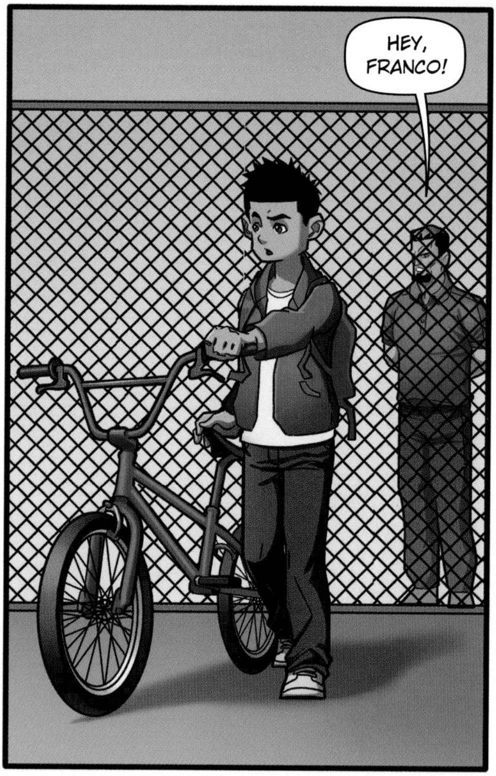
HEY, FRANCO!

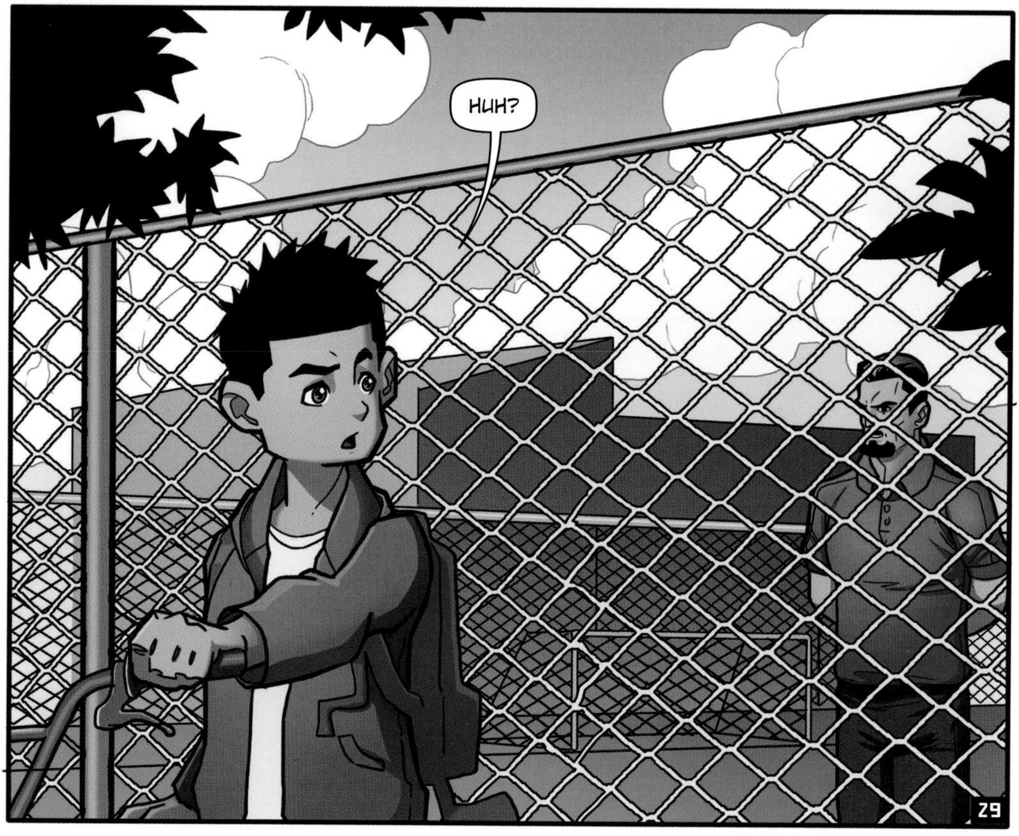
HUH?

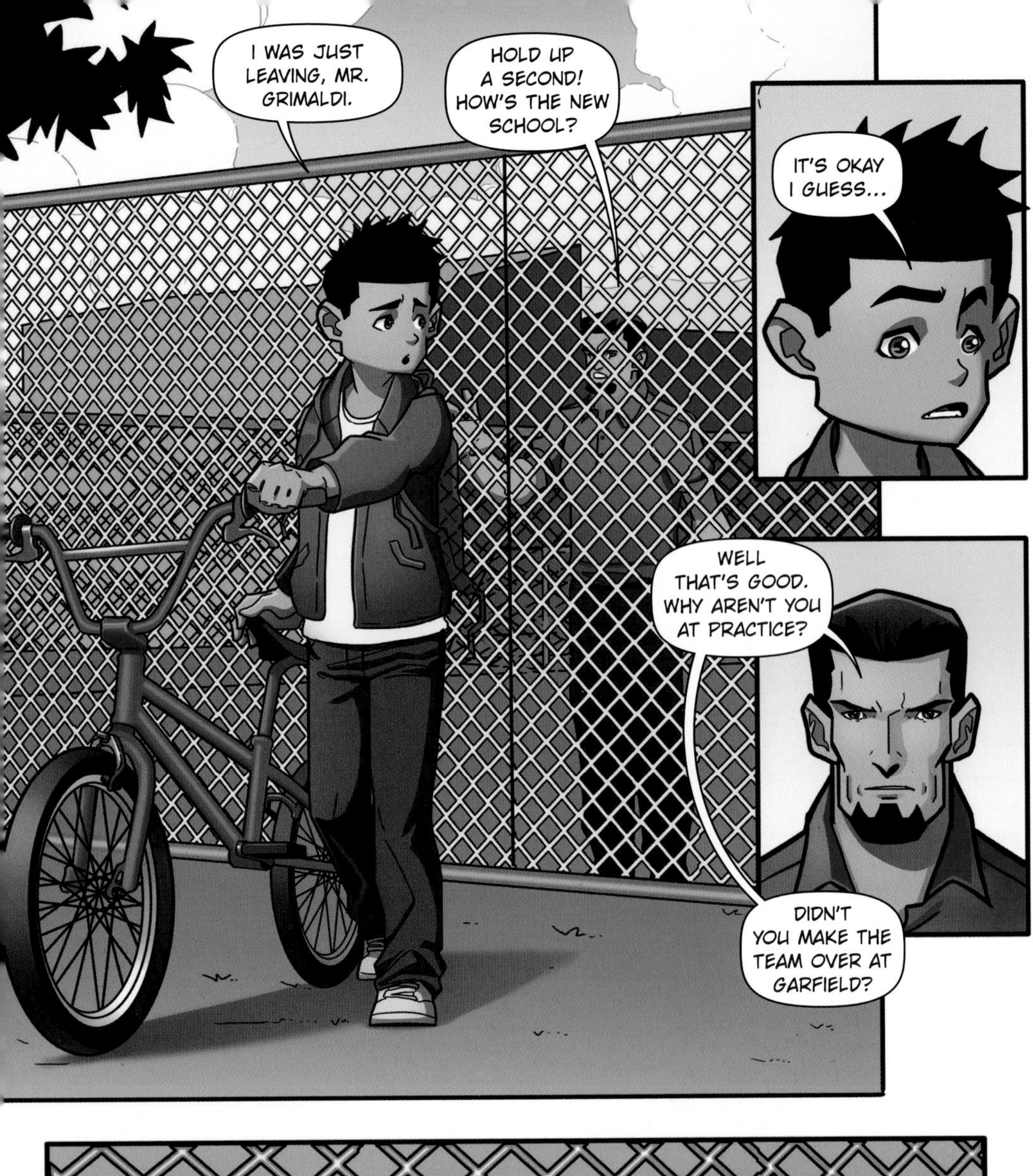
I WAS JUST LEAVING, MR. GRIMALDI.
HOLD UP A SECOND! HOW'S THE NEW SCHOOL?
IT'S OKAY I GUESS...
WELL THAT'S GOOD. WHY AREN'T YOU AT PRACTICE?
DIDN'T YOU MAKE THE TEAM OVER AT GARFIELD?

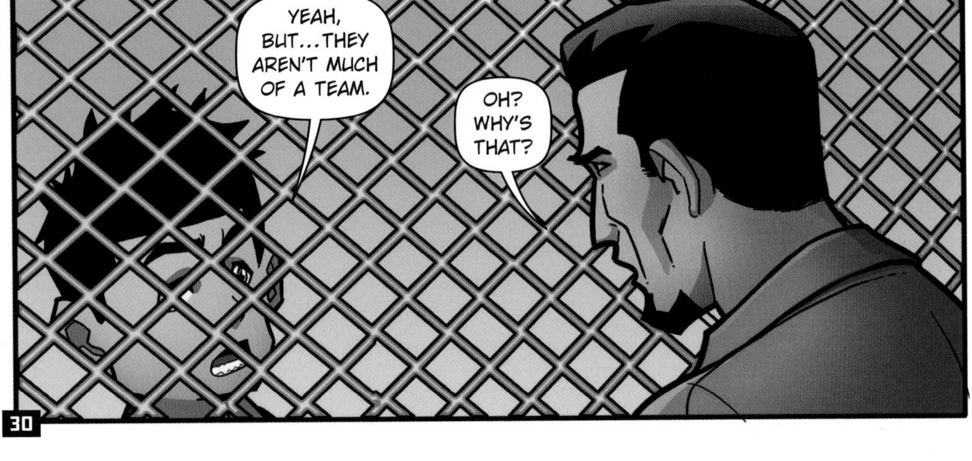
YEAH, BUT...THEY AREN'T MUCH OF A TEAM.
OH? WHY'S THAT?

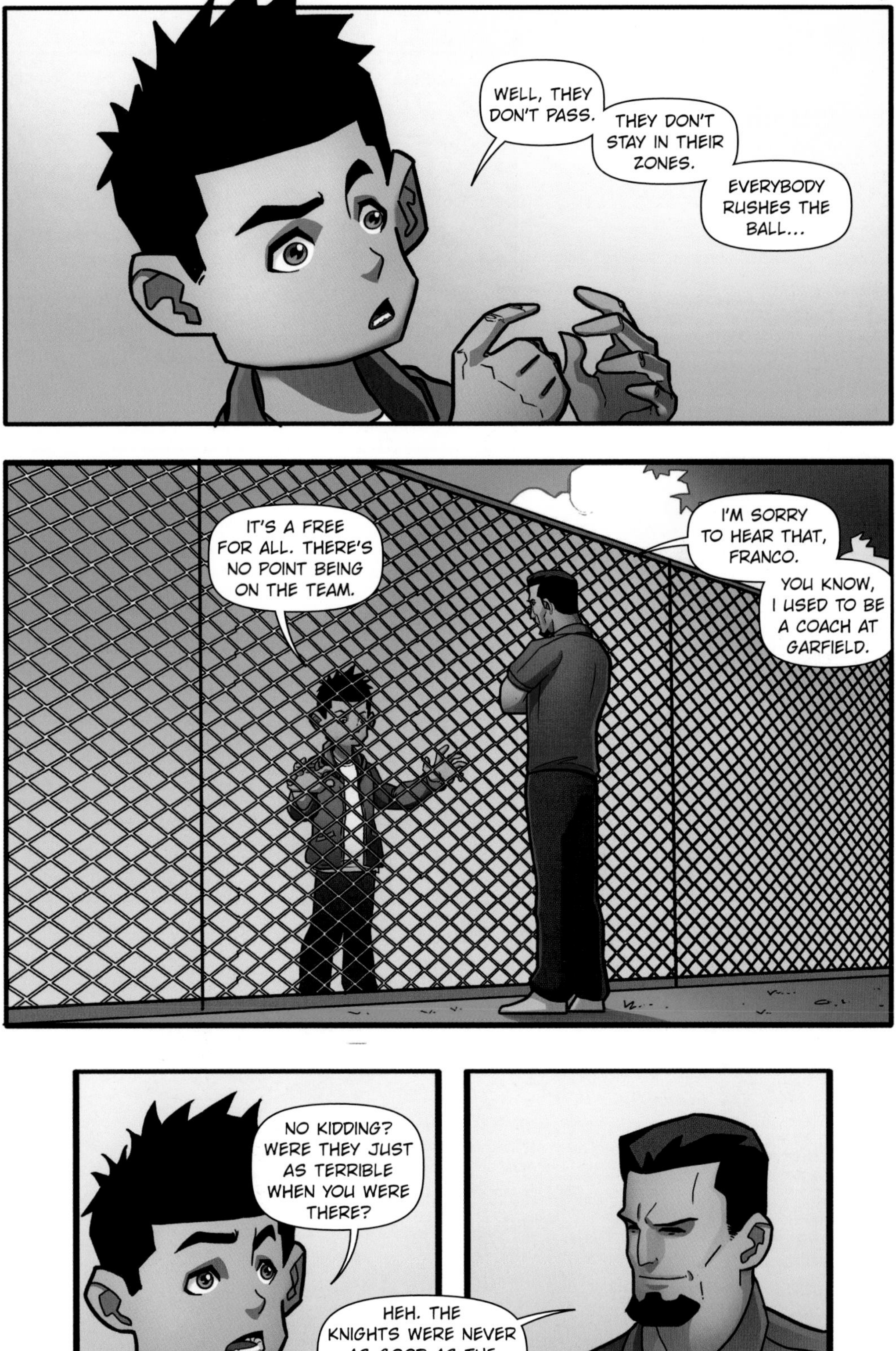
WELL, THEY DON'T PASS.
THEY DON'T STAY IN THEIR ZONES.
EVERYBODY RUSHES THE BALL...
IT'S A FREE FOR ALL. THERE'S NO POINT BEING ON THE TEAM.
I'M SORRY TO HEAR THAT, FRANCO.
YOU KNOW, I USED TO BE A COACH AT GARFIELD.
NO KIDDING? WERE THEY JUST AS TERRIBLE WHEN YOU WERE THERE?
HEH. THE KNIGHTS WERE NEVER AS GOOD AS THE BEARS ARE, BUT THEY WEREN'T TERRIBLE.

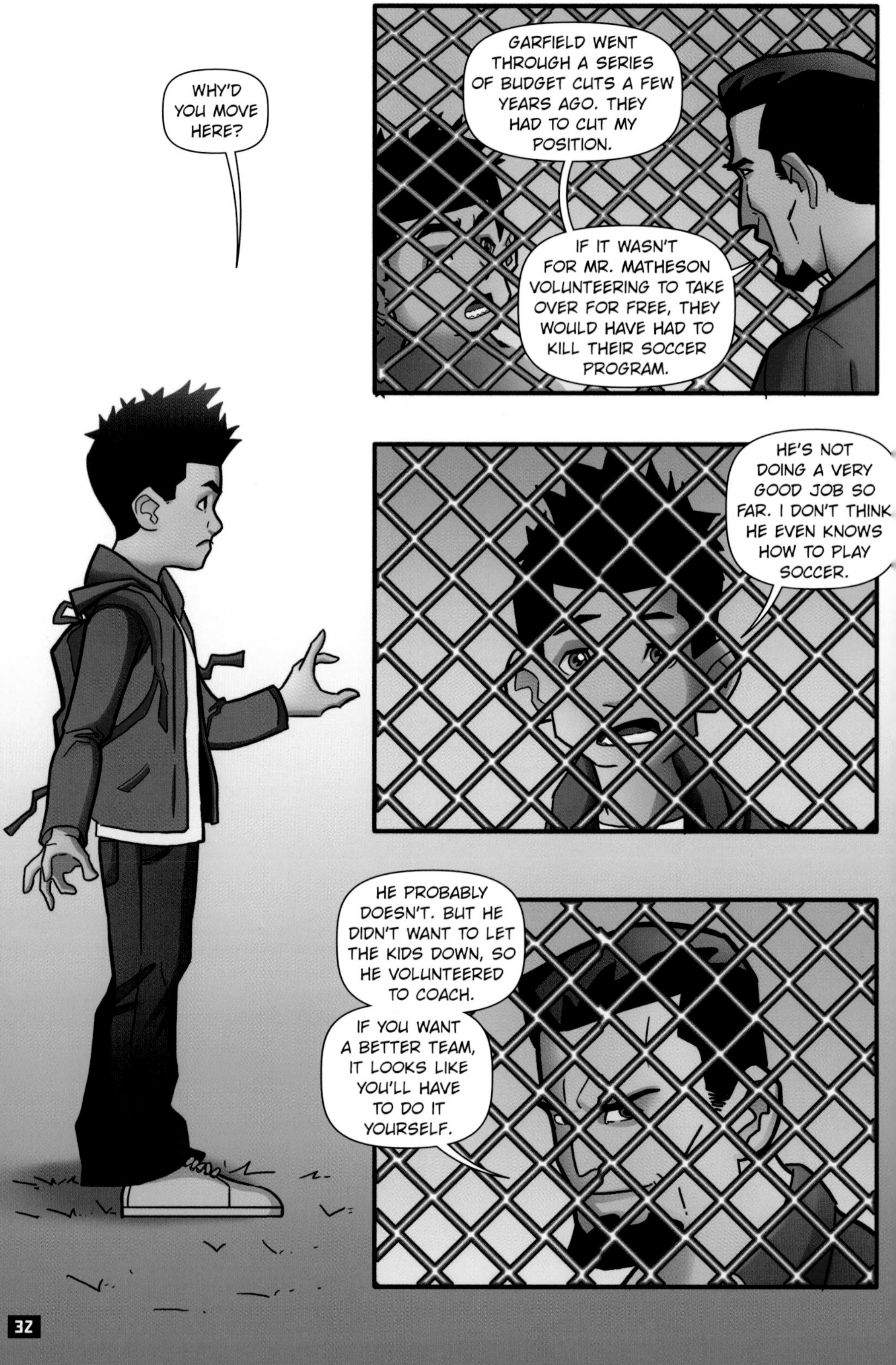
WHY'D YOU MOVE HERE?
GARFIELD WENT THROUGH A SERIES OF BUDGET CUTS A FEW YEARS AGO. THEY HAD TO CUT MY POSITION.
IF IT WASN'T FOR MR. MATHESON VOLUNTEERING TO TAKE OVER FOR FREE, THEY WOULD HAVE HAD TO KILL THEIR SOCCER PROGRAM.
HE'S NOT DOING A VERY GOOD JOB SO FAR. I DON'T THINK HE EVEN KNOWS HOW TO PLAY SOCCER.
HE PROBABLY DOESN'T. BUT HE DIDN'T WANT TO LET THE KIDS DOWN, SO HE VOLUNTEERED TO COACH.
IF YOU WANT A BETTER TEAM, IT LOOKS LIKE YOU'LL HAVE TO DO IT YOURSELF.

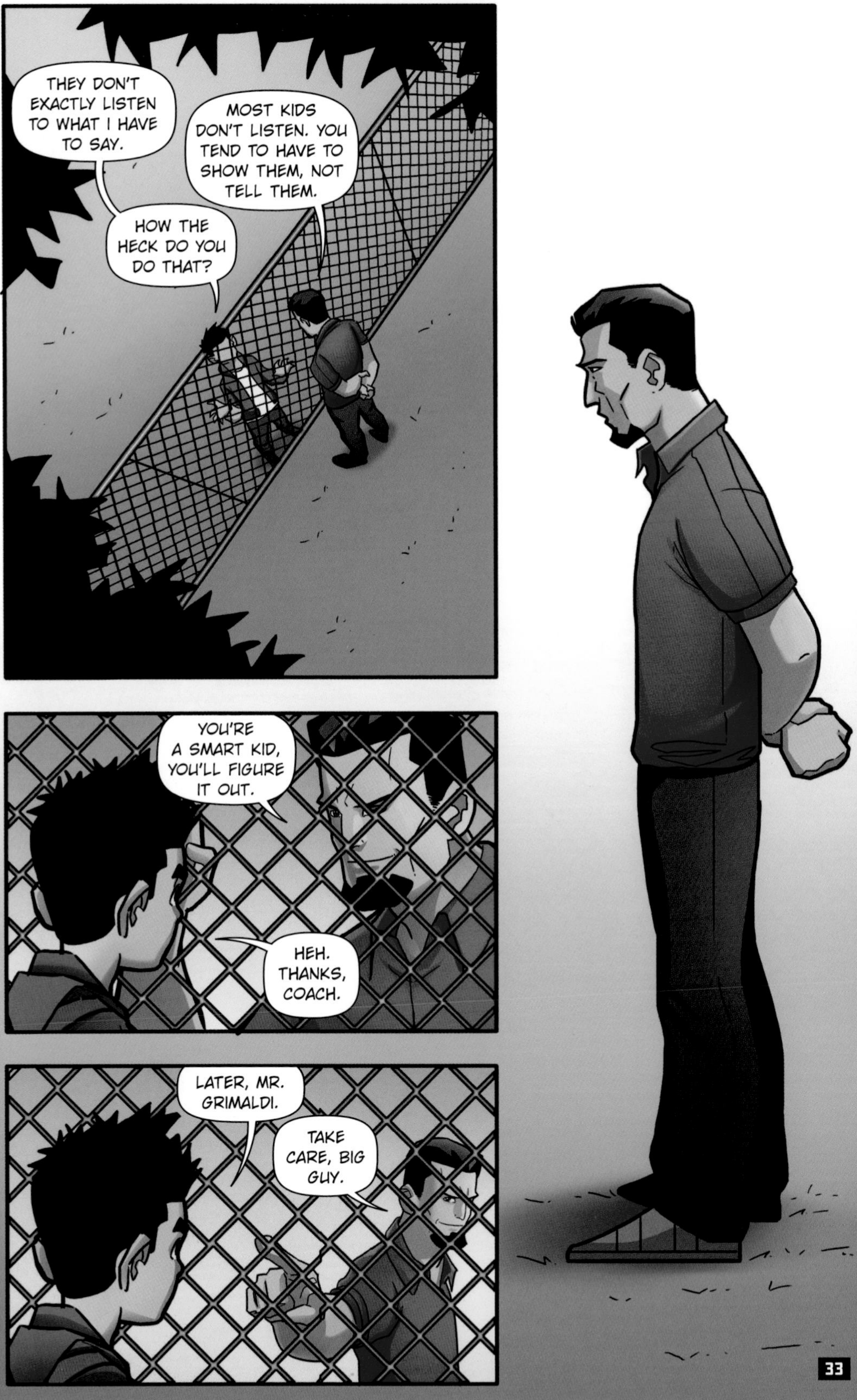
THEY DON'T EXACTLY LISTEN TO WHAT I HAVE TO SAY.
MOST KIDS DON'T LISTEN. YOU TEND TO HAVE TO SHOW THEM, NOT TELL THEM.
HOW THE HECK DO YOU DO THAT?
YOU'RE A SMART KID, YOU'LL FIGURE IT OUT.
HEH. THANKS, COACH.
LATER, MR. GRIMALDI.
TAKE CARE, BIG GUY.

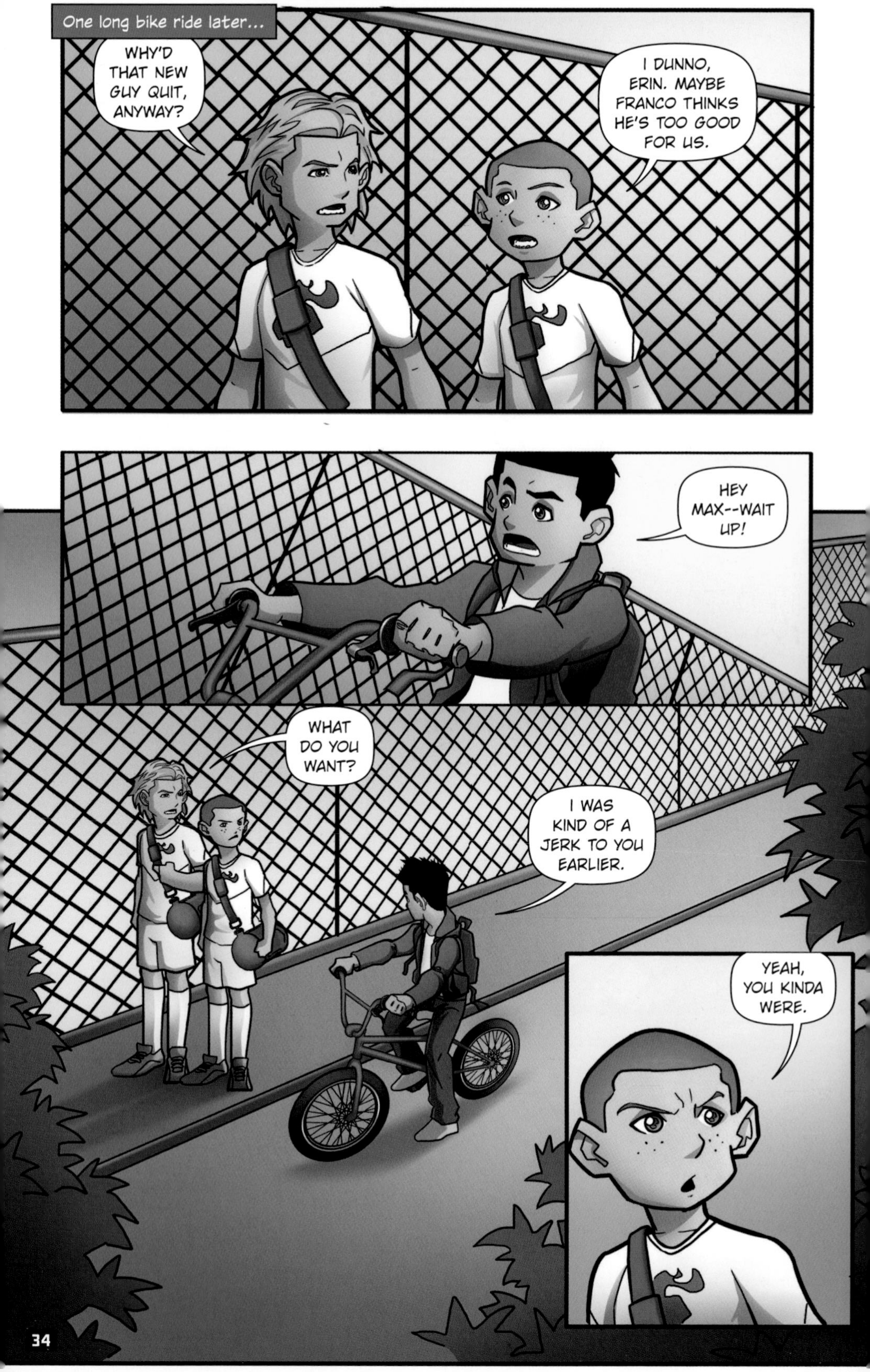
One long bike ride later...
WHY'D THAT NEW GUY QUIT, ANYWAY?
I DUNNO, ERIN. MAYBE FRANCO THINKS HE'S TOO GOOD FOR US.
HEY MAX--WAIT UP!
WHAT DO YOU WANT?
I WAS KIND OF A JERK TO YOU EARLIER.
YEAH, YOU KINDA WERE.

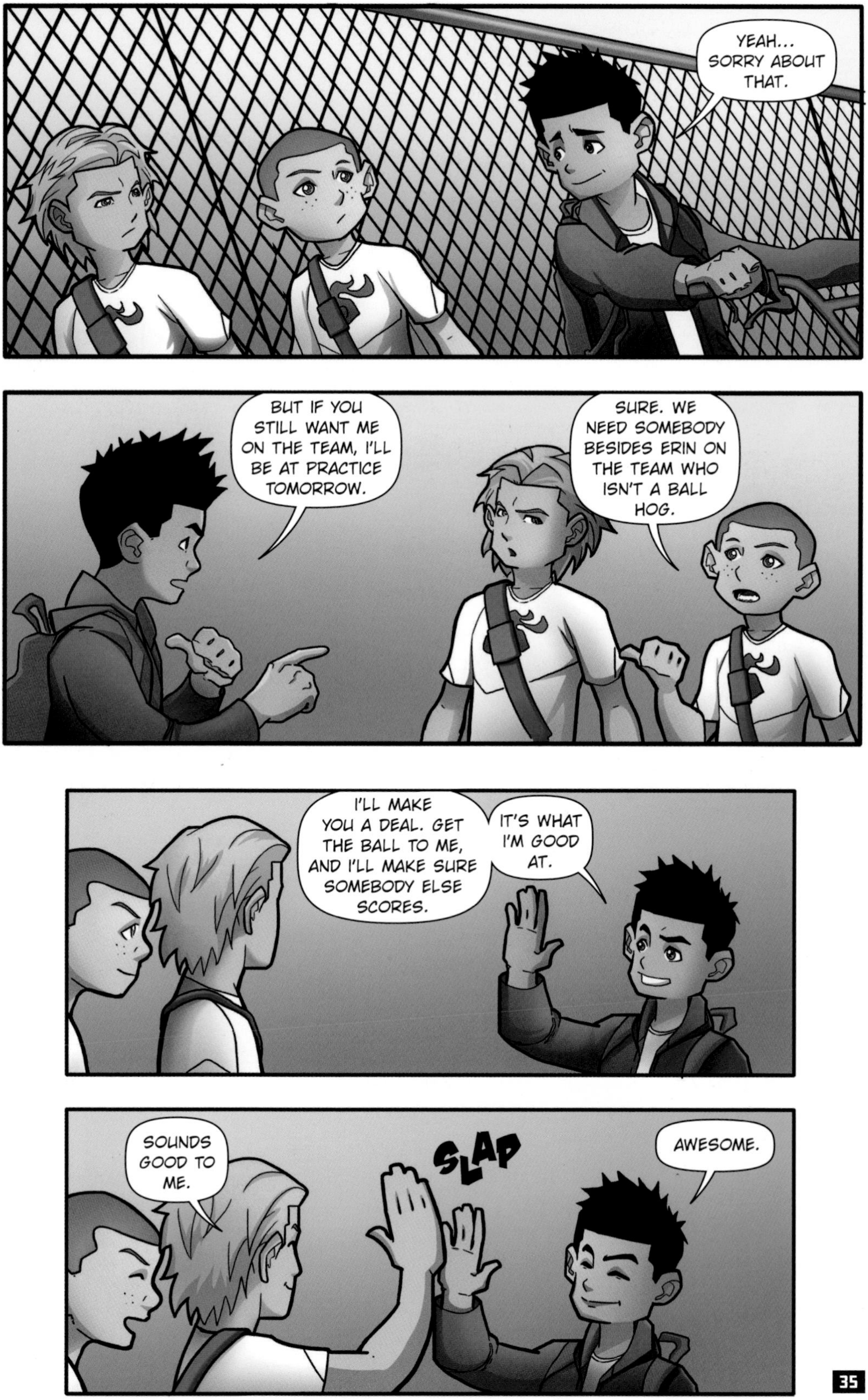
YEAH... SORRY ABOUT THAT.
BUT IF YOU STILL WANT ME ON THE TEAM, I'LL BE AT PRACTICE TOMORROW.
SURE. WE NEED SOMEBODY BESIDES ERIN ON THE TEAM WHO ISN'T A BALL HOG.
I'LL MAKE YOU A DEAL. GET THE BALL TO ME, AND I'LL MAKE SURE SOMEBODY ELSE SCORES.
IT'S WHAT I'M GOOD AT.
SOUNDS GOOD TO ME.
SLAP
AWESOME.

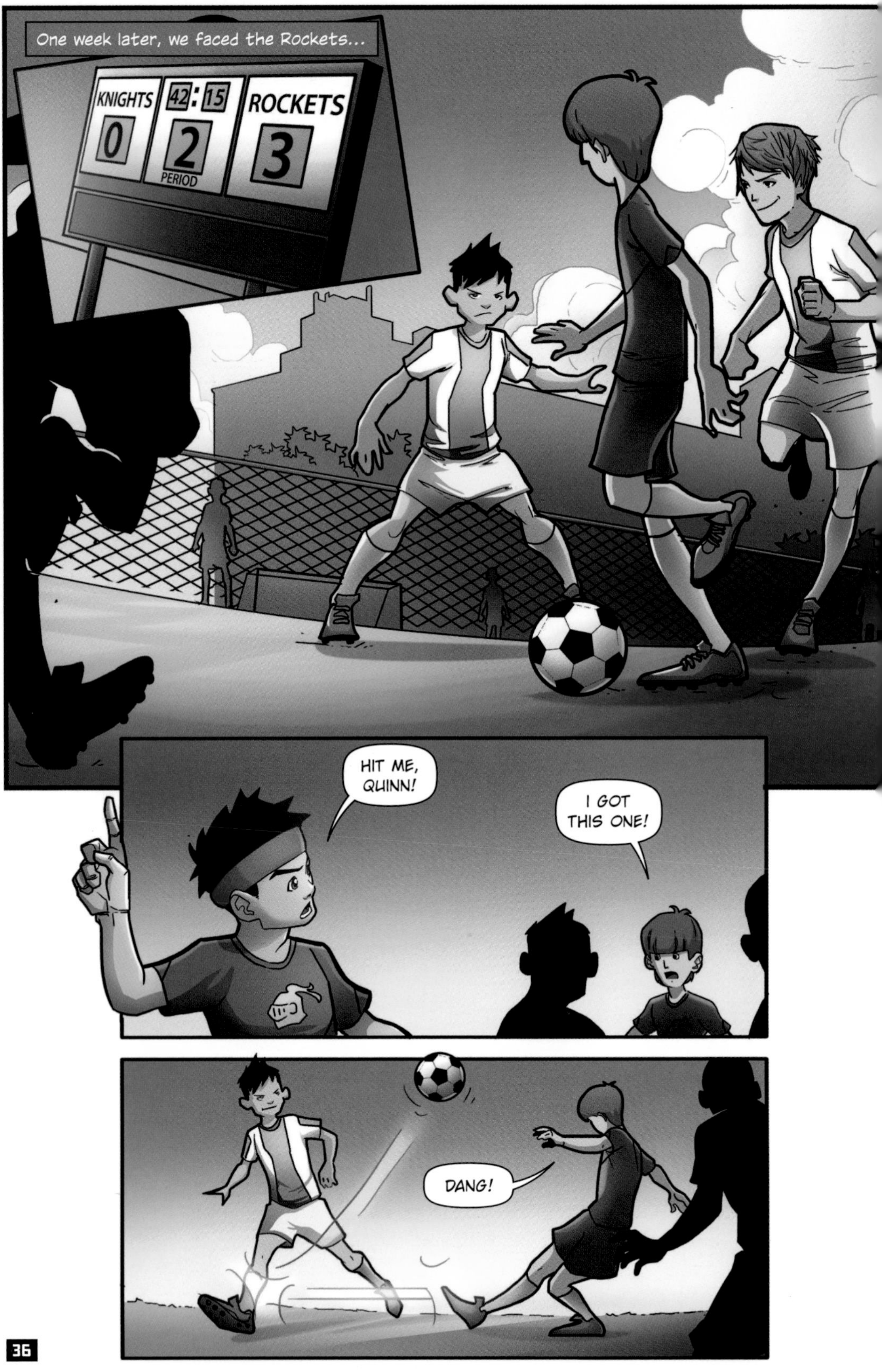

One week later, we faced the Rockets...
KNIGHTS 0
42:15
2 PERIOD
ROCKETS 3
HIT ME, QUINN!
I GOT THIS ONE!
DANG!

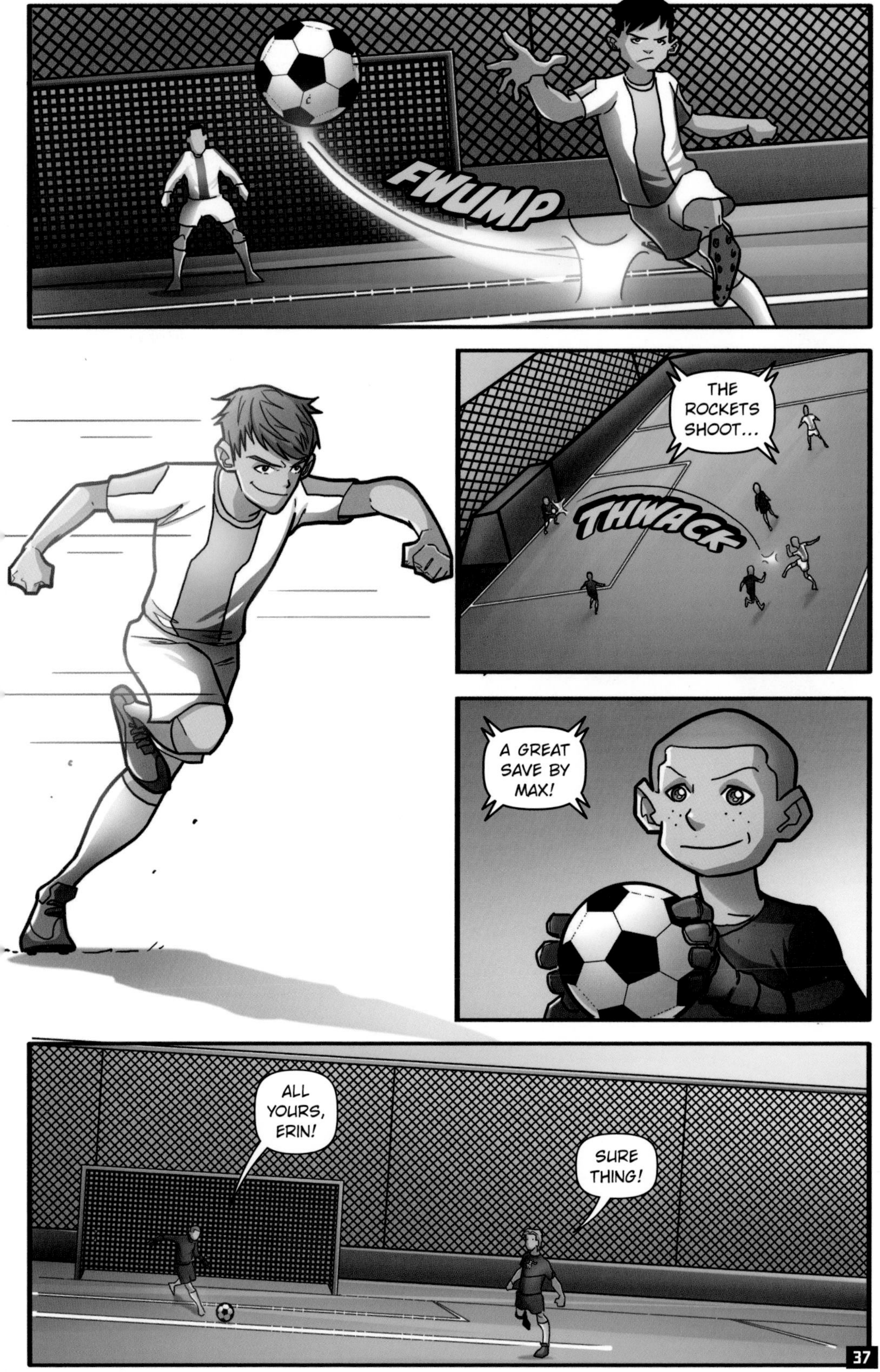
FWUMP
THE ROCKETS SHOOT...
THWACK
A GREAT SAVE BY MAX!
ALL YOURS, ERIN!
SURE THING!

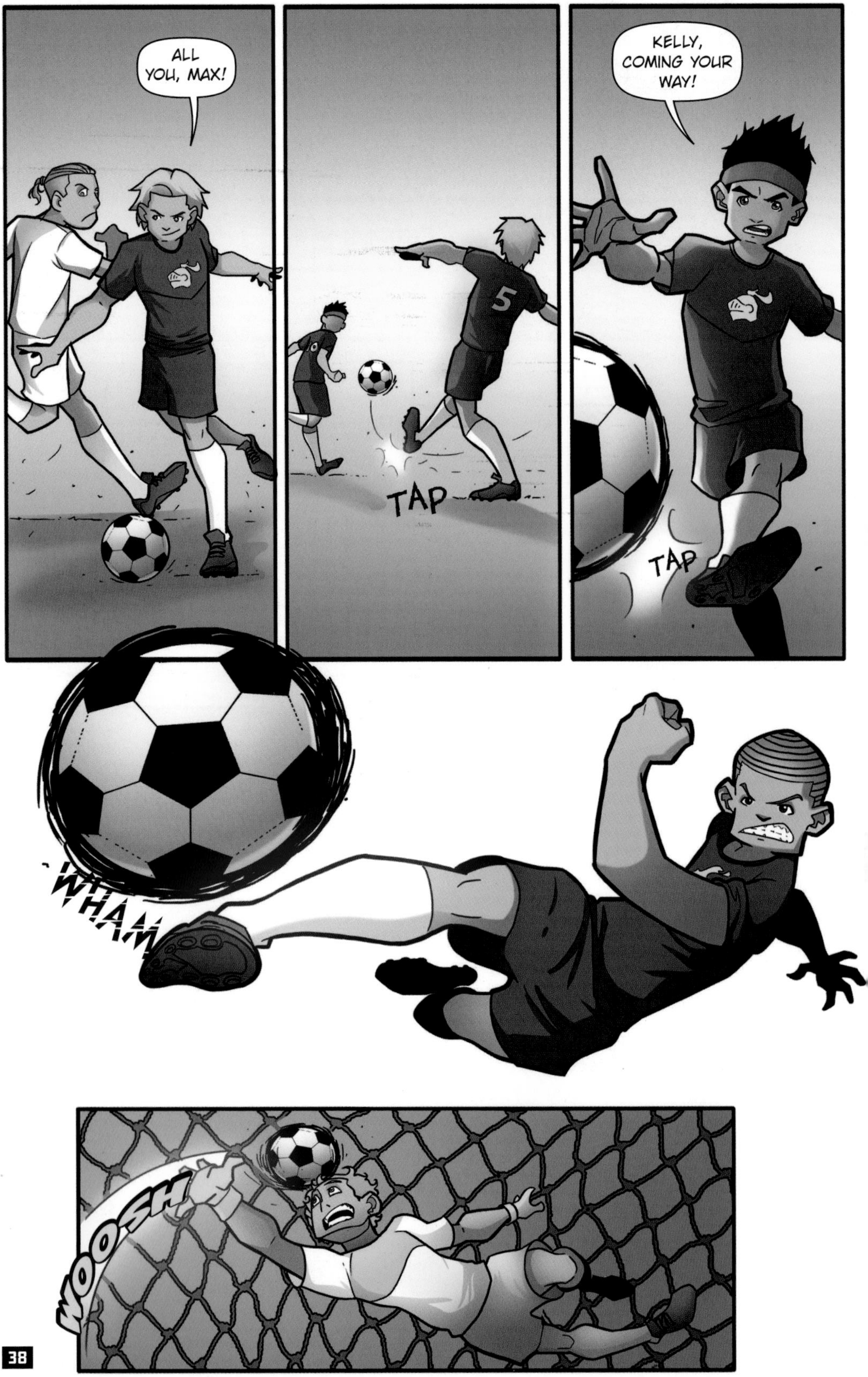

ALL YOU, MAX!
TAP
KELLY, COMING YOUR WAY!
TAP
WHAM
WOOSH

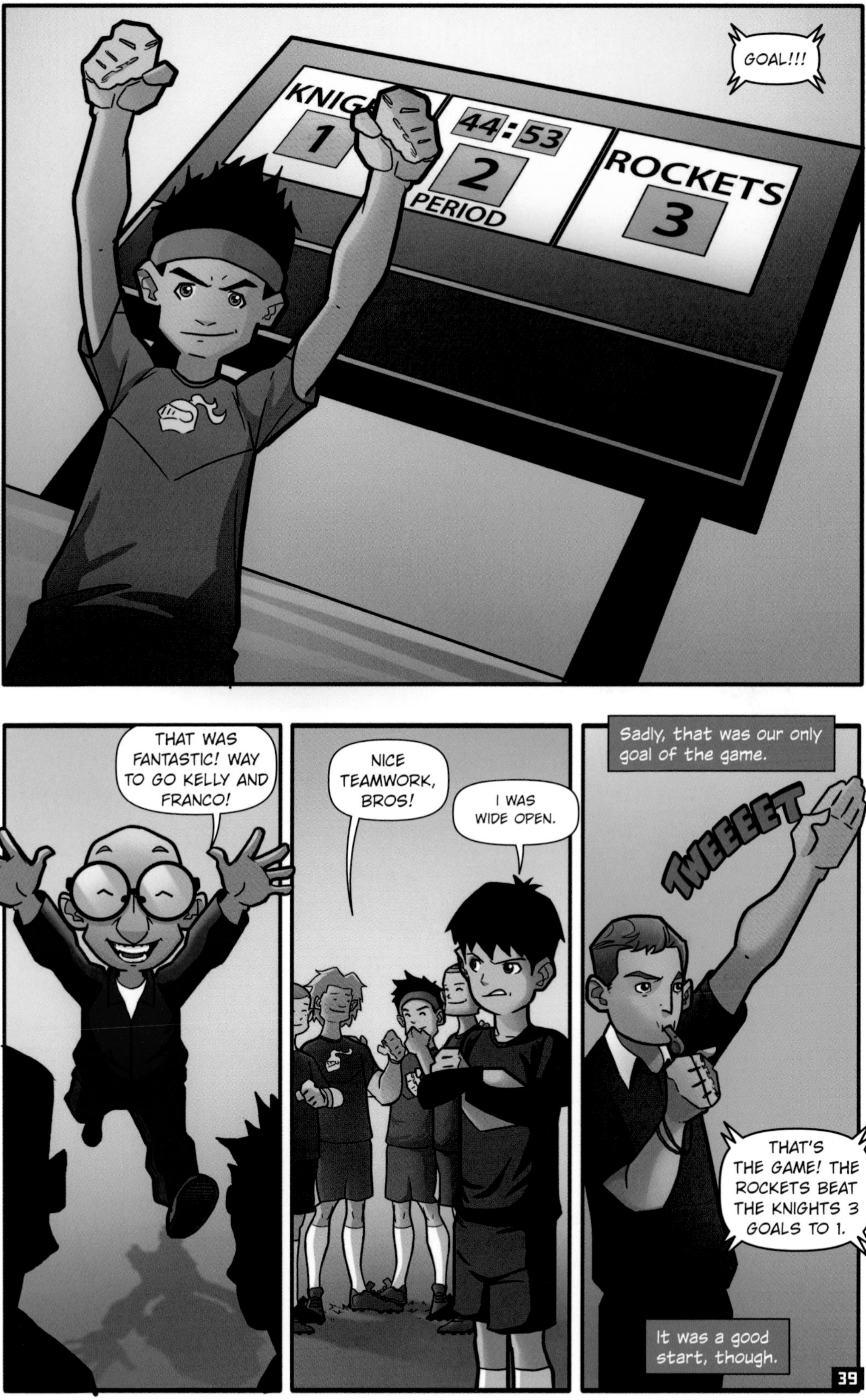
GOAL!!!
KNIG
1
44:53
2
PERIOD
ROCKETS
3
THAT WAS FANTASTIC! WAY TO GO KELLY AND FRANCO!
NICE TEAMWORK, BROS!
I WAS WIDE OPEN.
Sadly, that was our only goal of the game.
TWEEEET
THAT'S THE GAME! THE ROCKETS BEAT THE KNIGHTS 3 GOALS TO 1.
It was a good start, though.

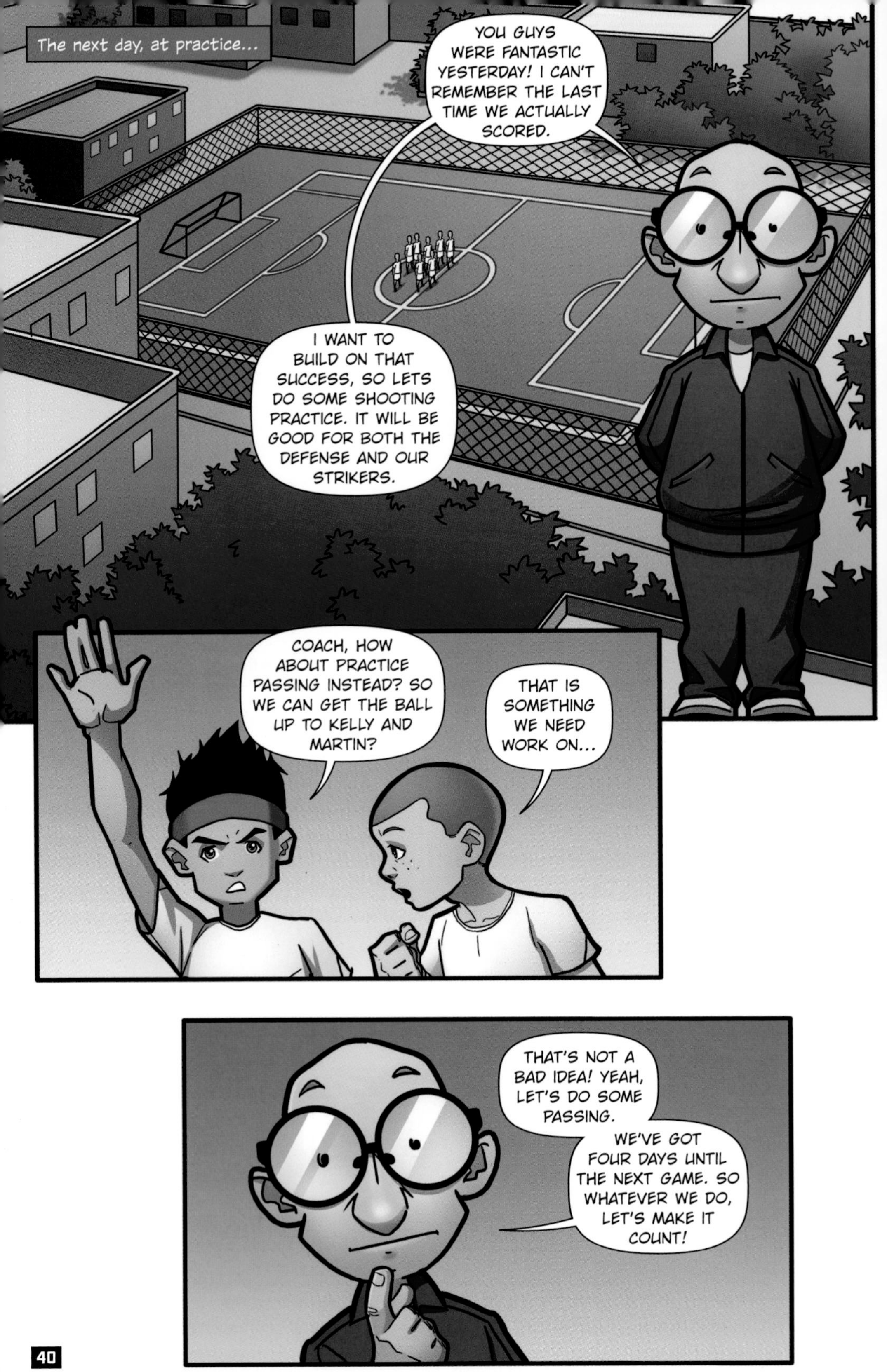
The next day, at practice...
YOU GUYS WERE FANTASTIC YESTERDAY! I CAN'T REMEMBER THE LAST TIME WE ACTUALLY SCORED.
I WANT TO BUILD ON THAT SUCCESS, SO LETS DO SOME SHOOTING PRACTICE. IT WILL BE GOOD FOR BOTH THE DEFENSE AND OUR STRIKERS.
COACH, HOW ABOUT PRACTICE PASSING INSTEAD? SO WE CAN GET THE BALL UP TO KELLY AND MARTIN?
THAT IS SOMETHING WE NEED WORK ON...
THAT'S NOT A BAD IDEA! YEAH, LET'S DO SOME PASSING.
WE'VE GOT FOUR DAYS UNTIL THE NEXT GAME. SO WHATEVER WE DO, LET'S MAKE IT COUNT!

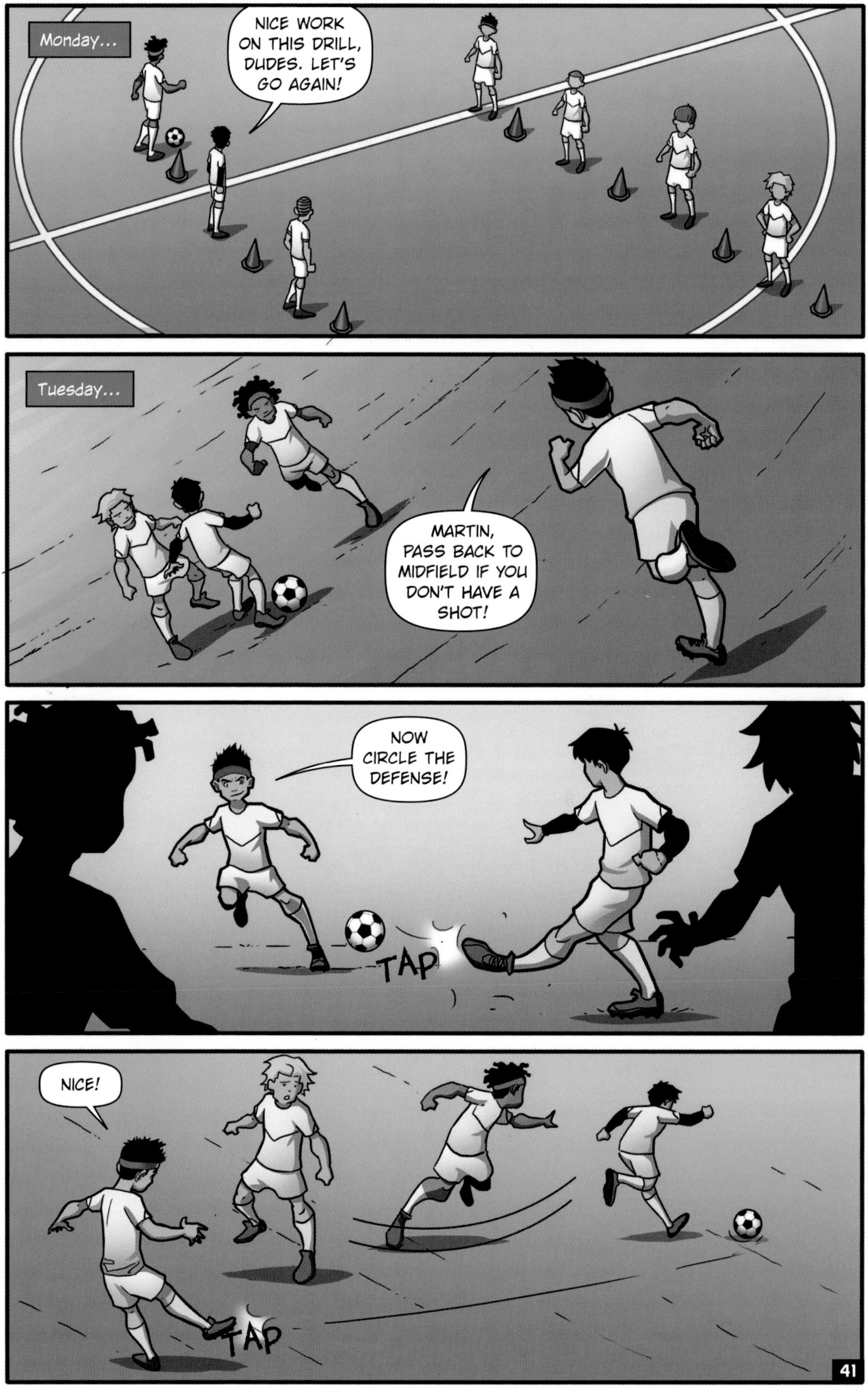
Monday...
NICE WORK ON THIS DRILL, DUDES. LET'S GO AGAIN!
Tuesday...
MARTIN, PASS BACK TO MIDFIELD IF YOU DON'T HAVE A SHOT!
NOW CIRCLE THE DEFENSE!
TAP
NICE!
TAP

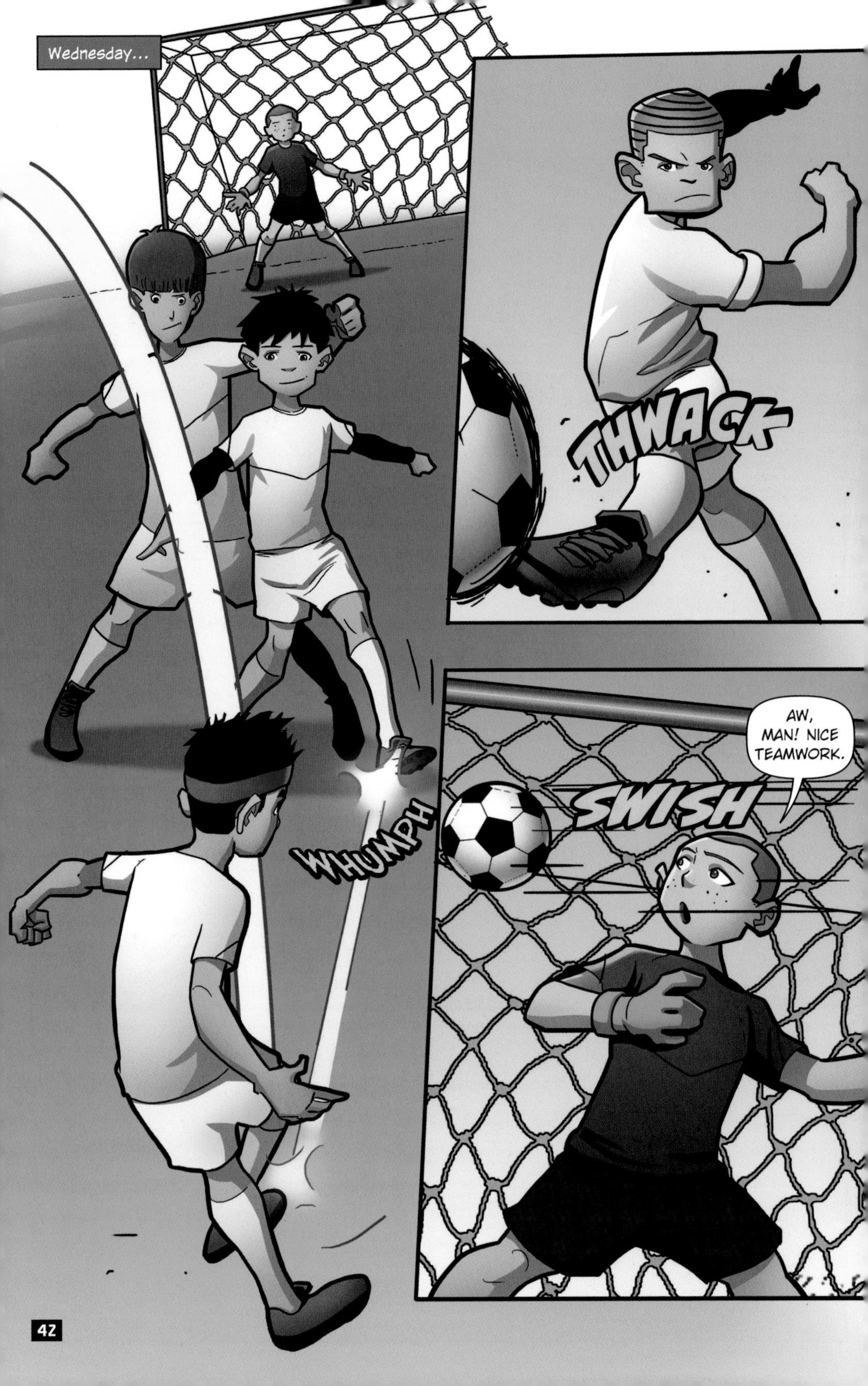
Wednesday...
WHUMPH
THWACK
SWISH
AW, MAN! NICE TEAMWORK.

Thursday...

GREAT PRACTICE, GUYS! BRING IT IN.

IT'S HARD [TO] BELIEVE THIS [IS] THE SAME TEAM [WE] HAD A FEW [W]EEKS AGO.

I HAVE TO TELL YOU, I'M REALLY LOOKING FORWARD TO SEEING YOUR NEW TEAMWORK TOMORROW AGAINST THE CARTER BEARS.

SO GO HOME AND GET SOME REST. I'LL SEE YOU ALL TOMORROW.

MY OLD TEAM...

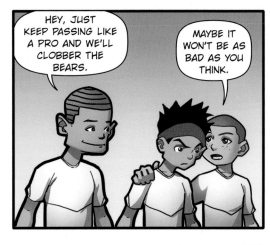

HEY, JUST KEEP PASSING LIKE A PRO AND WE'LL CLOBBER THE BEARS.

MAYBE IT WON'T BE AS BAD AS YOU THINK.

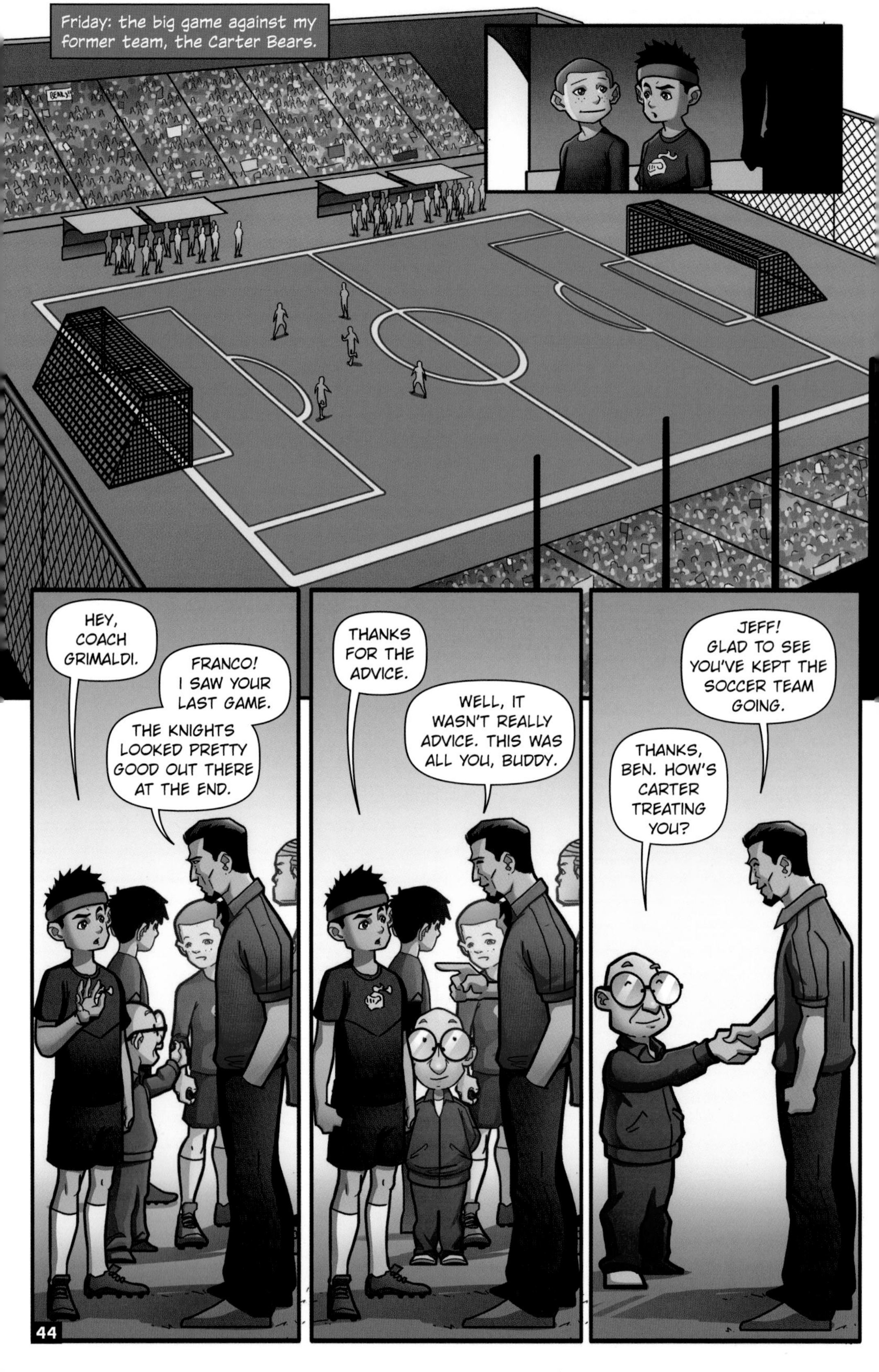
Friday: the big game against my former team, the Carter Bears.
HEY, COACH GRIMALDI.
FRANCO! I SAW YOUR LAST GAME.
THE KNIGHTS LOOKED PRETTY GOOD OUT THERE AT THE END.
THANKS FOR THE ADVICE.
WELL, IT WASN'T REALLY ADVICE. THIS WAS ALL YOU, BUDDY.
JEFF! GLAD TO SEE YOU'VE KEPT THE SOCCER TEAM GOING.
THANKS, BEN. HOW'S CARTER TREATING YOU?

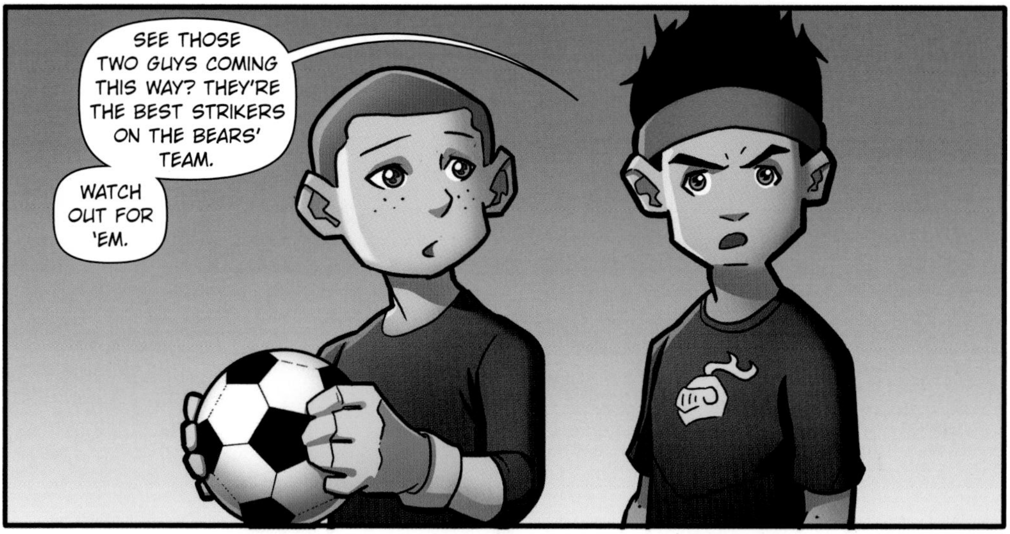
SEE THOSE TWO GUYS COMING THIS WAY? THEY'RE THE BEST STRIKERS ON THE BEARS' TEAM.
WATCH OUT FOR 'EM.

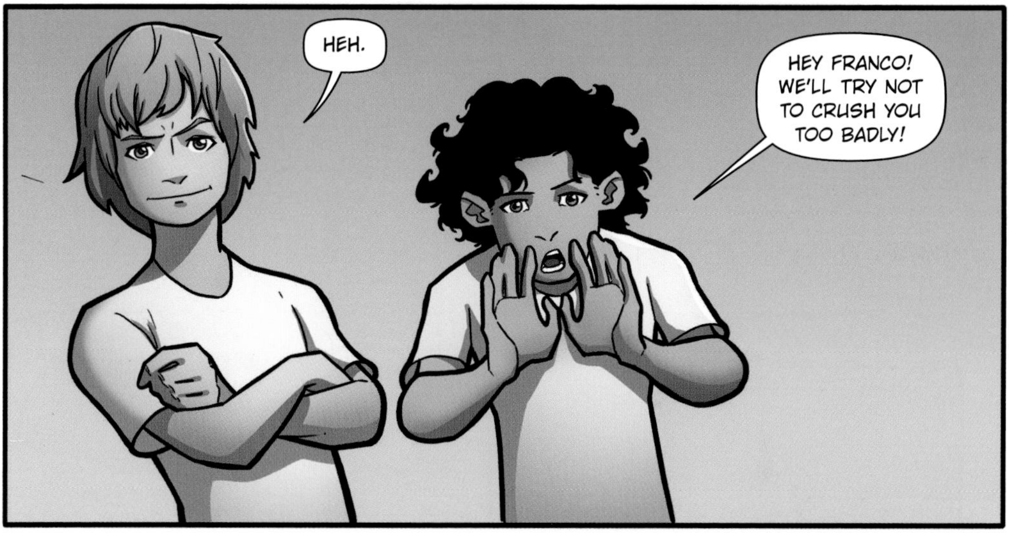
HEH.
HEY FRANCO! WE'LL TRY NOT TO CRUSH YOU TOO BADLY!

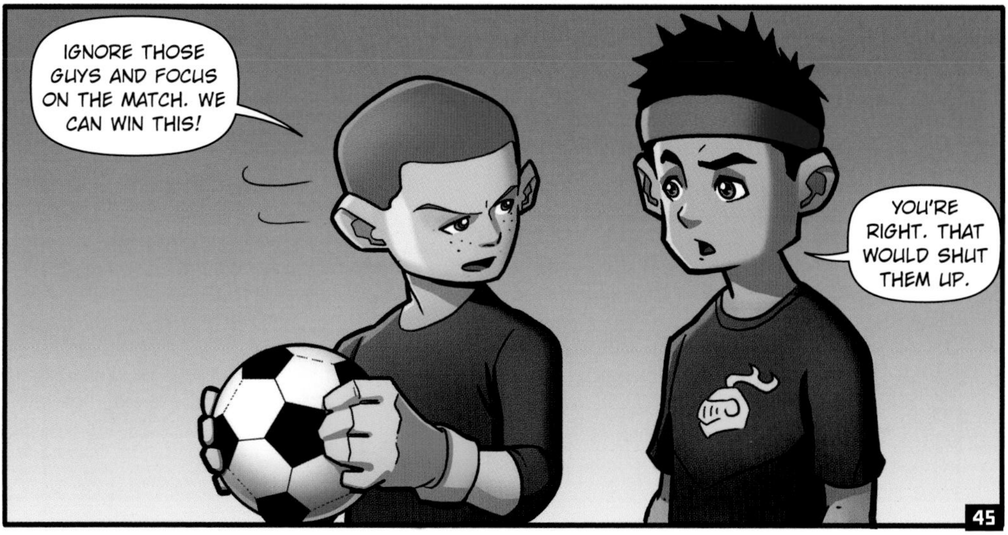
IGNORE THOSE GUYS AND FOCUS ON THE MATCH. WE CAN WIN THIS!
YOU'RE RIGHT. THAT WOULD SHUT THEM UP.

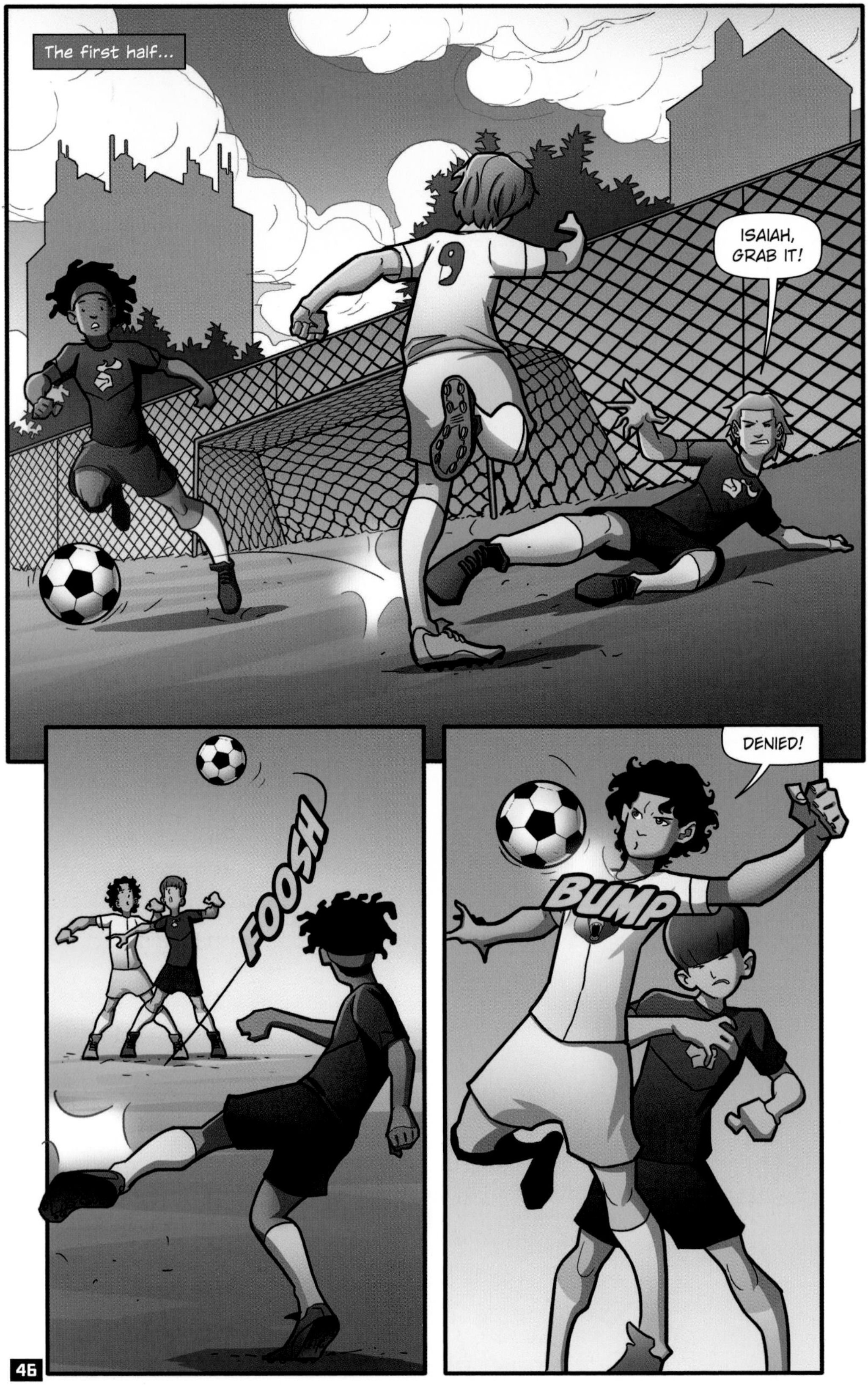
The first half...
ISAIAH, GRAB IT!
FOOSH
DENIED!
BUMP

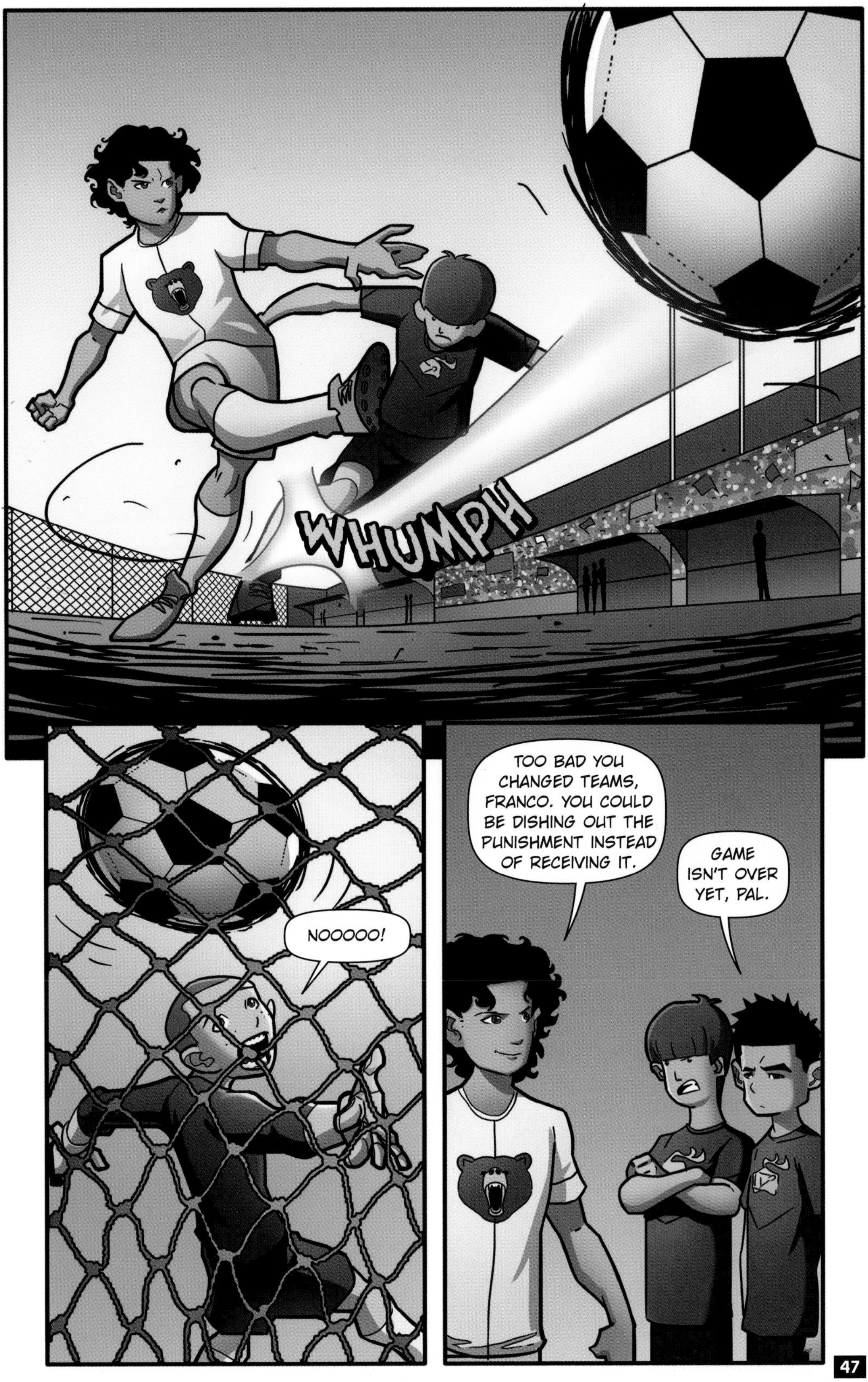
WHUMPH
NOOOOO!
TOO BAD YOU CHANGED TEAMS, FRANCO. YOU COULD BE DISHING OUT THE PUNISHMENT INSTEAD OF RECEIVING IT.
GAME ISN'T OVER YET, PAL.

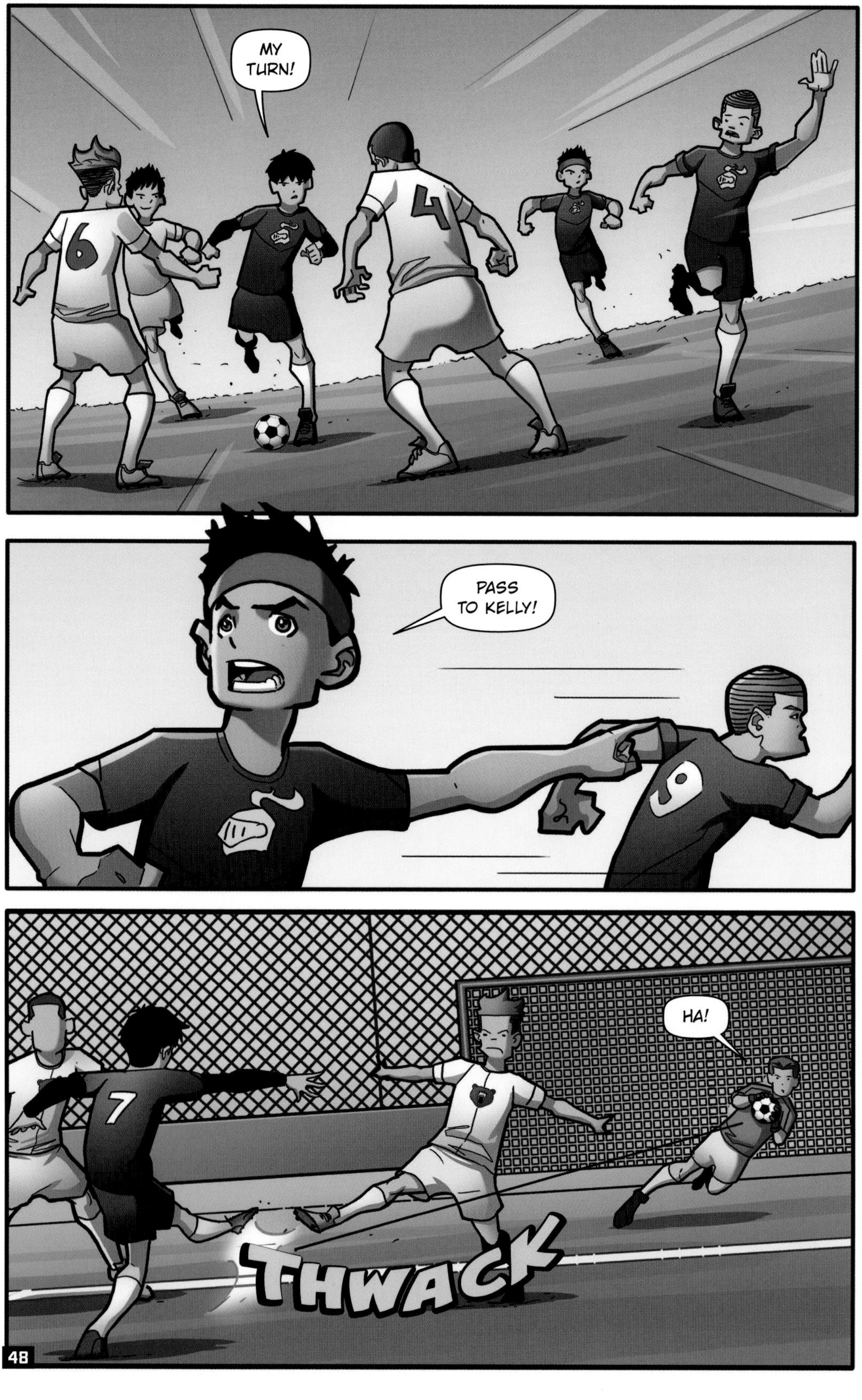
MY TURN!
PASS TO KELLY!
HA!
THWACK

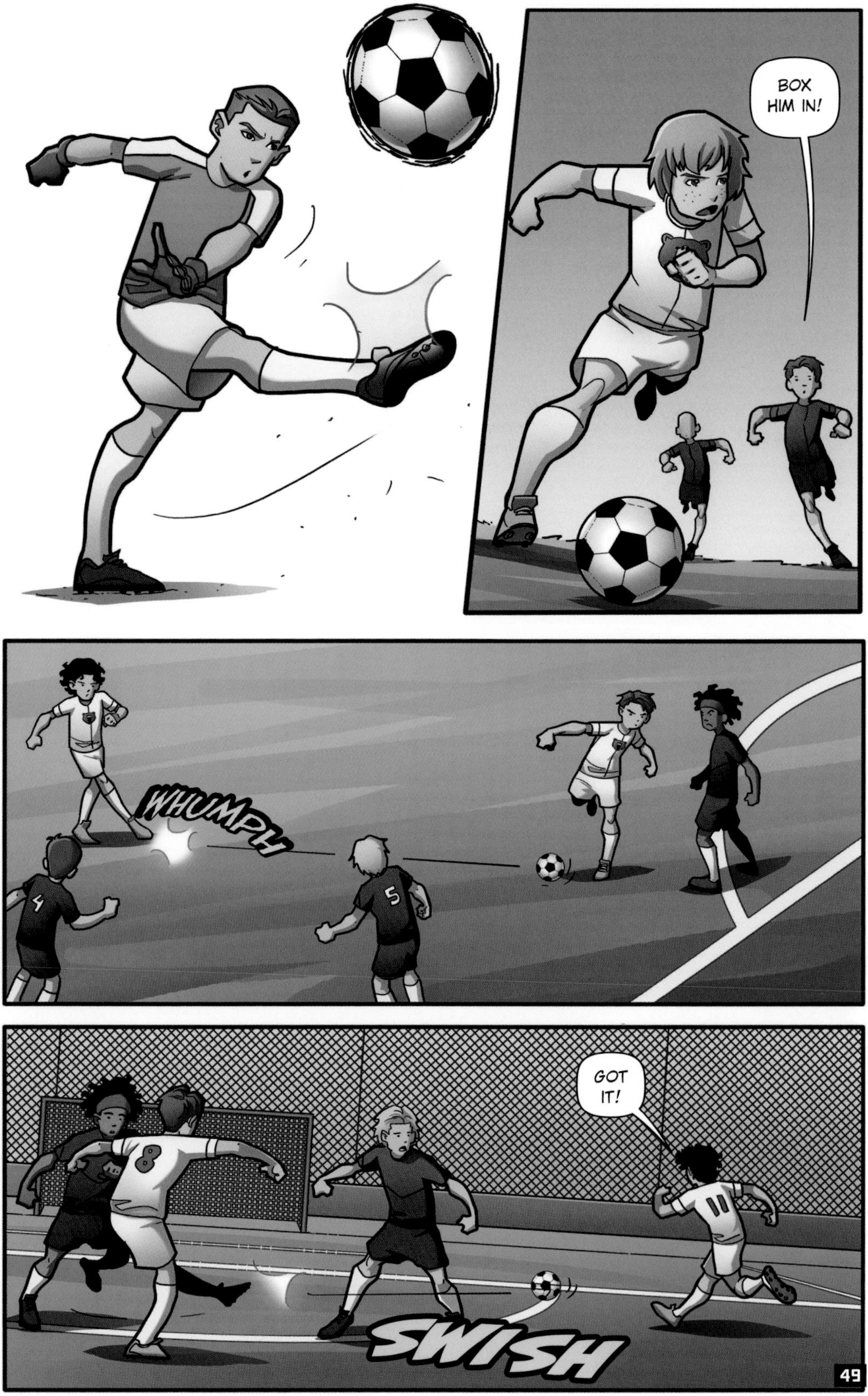
BOX HIM IN!
WHUMPH
GOT IT!
SWISH

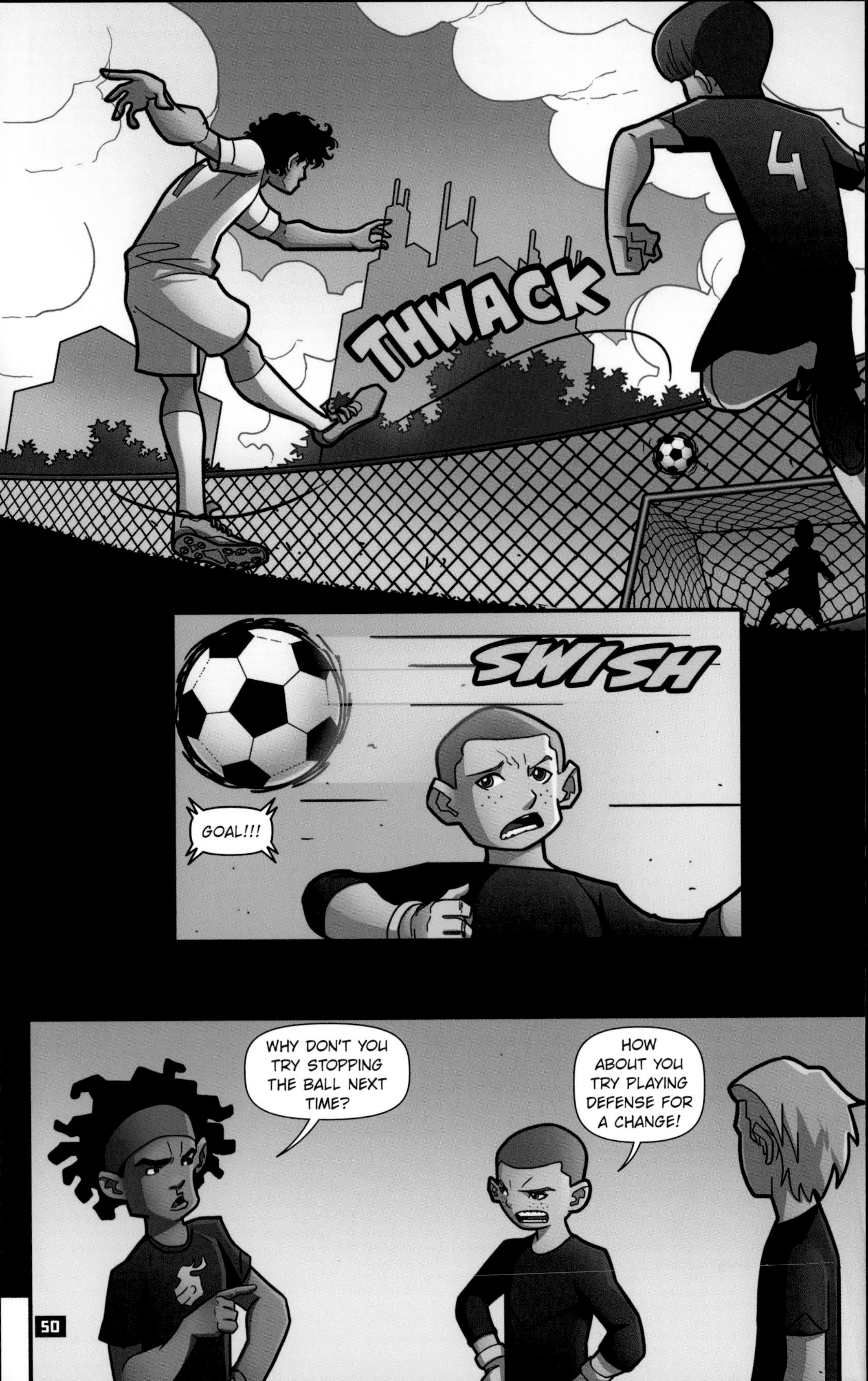
THWACK
SWISH
GOAL!!!
WHY DON'T YOU TRY STOPPING THE BALL NEXT TIME?
HOW ABOUT YOU TRY PLAYING DEFENSE FOR A CHANGE!

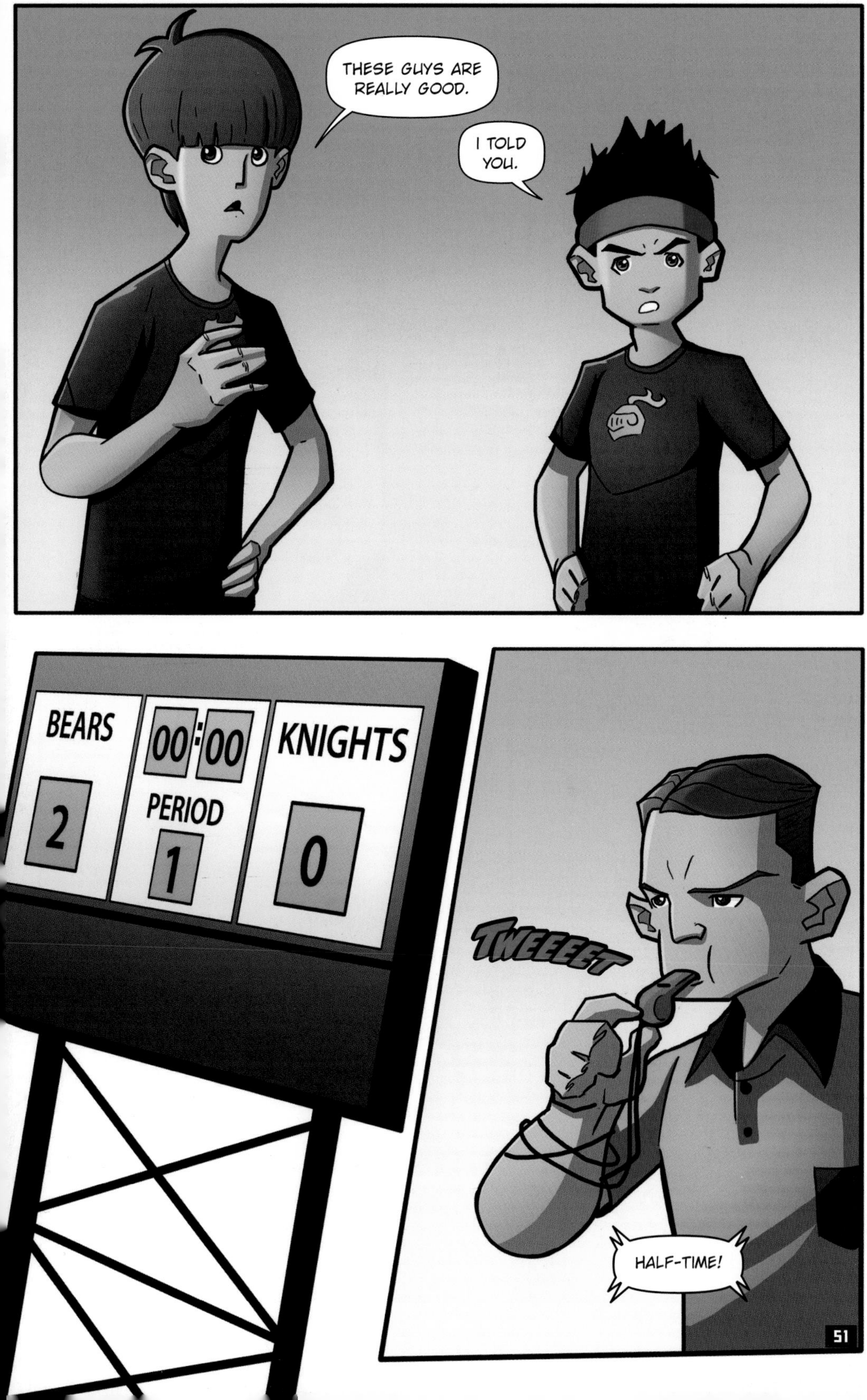
THESE GUYS ARE REALLY GOOD.
I TOLD YOU.
BEARS
00:00
KNIGHTS
2
PERIOD
1
0
TWEEEEET
HALF-TIME!

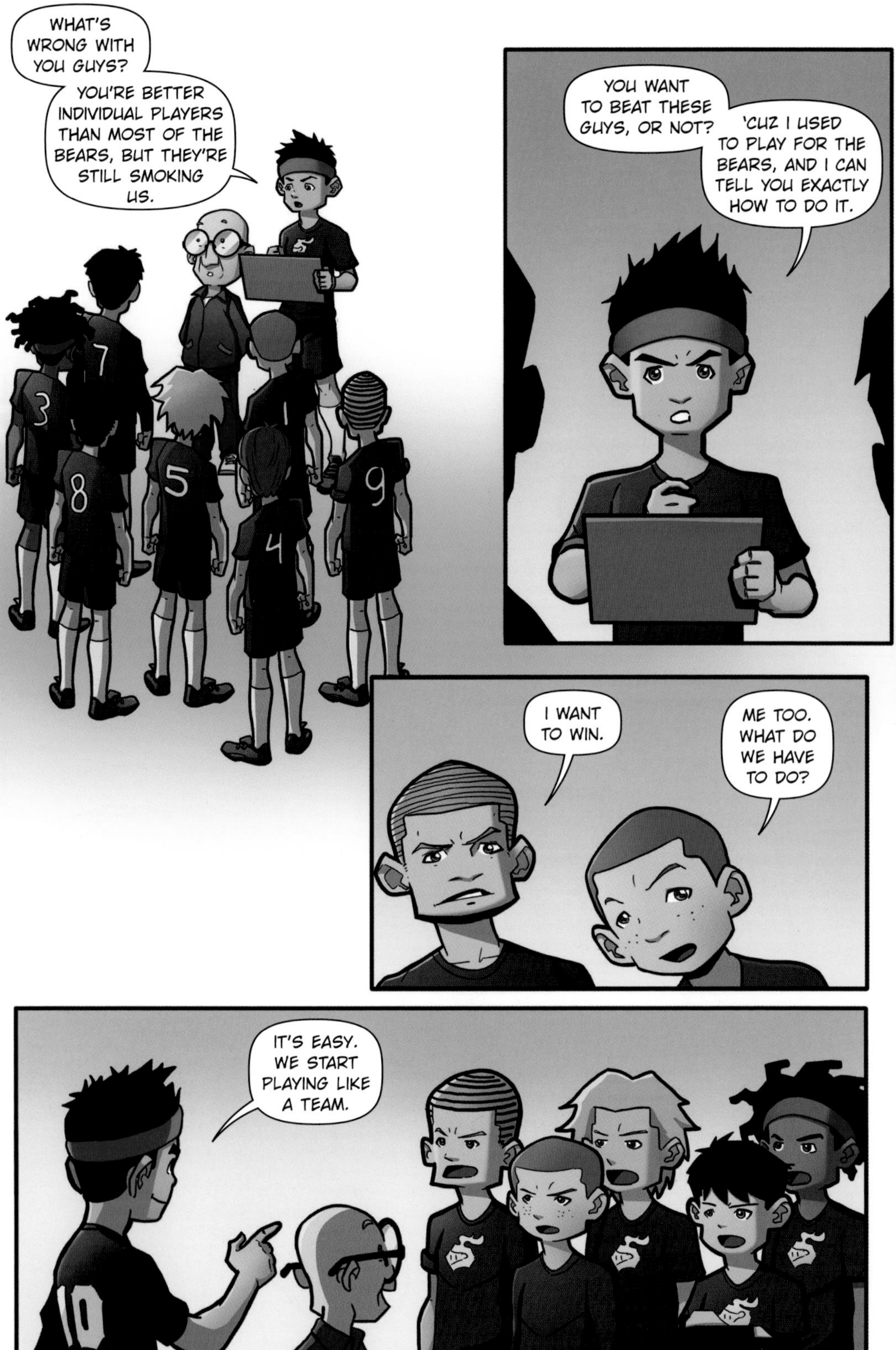
WHAT'S WRONG WITH YOU GUYS?
YOU'RE BETTER INDIVIDUAL PLAYERS THAN MOST OF THE BEARS, BUT THEY'RE STILL SMOKING US.
YOU WANT TO BEAT THESE GUYS, OR NOT?
'CUZ I USED TO PLAY FOR THE BEARS, AND I CAN TELL YOU EXACTLY HOW TO DO IT.
I WANT TO WIN.
ME TOO. WHAT DO WE HAVE TO DO?
IT'S EASY. WE START PLAYING LIKE A TEAM.

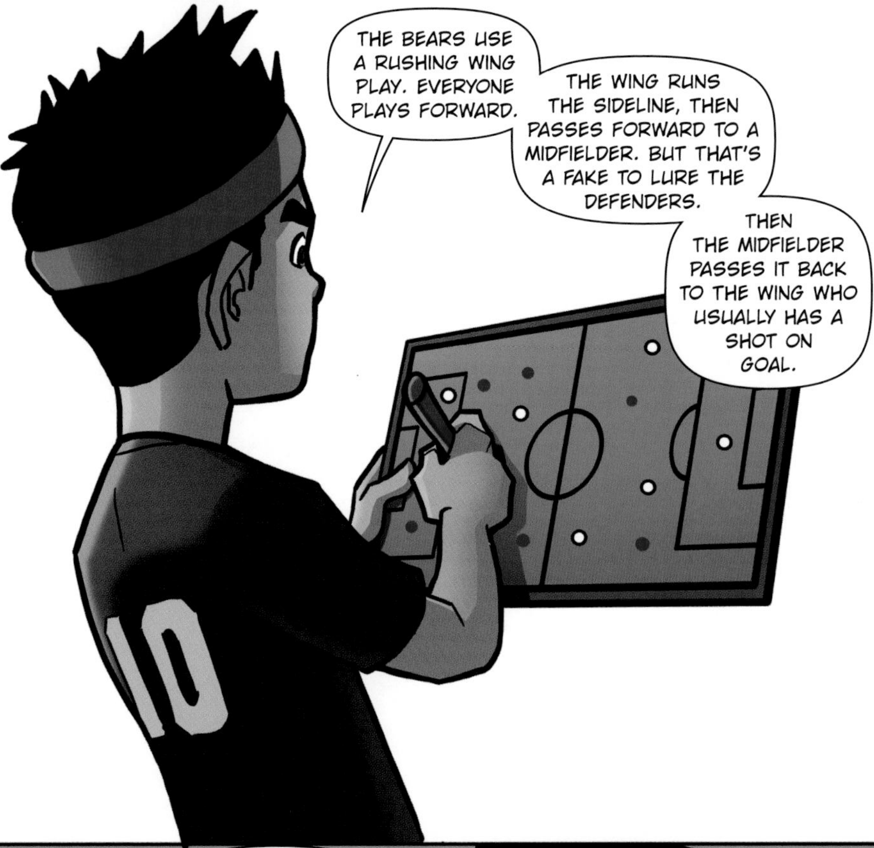
THE BEARS USE A RUSHING WING PLAY. EVERYONE PLAYS FORWARD.
THE WING RUNS THE SIDELINE, THEN PASSES FORWARD TO A MIDFIELDER. BUT THAT'S A FAKE TO LURE THE DEFENDERS.
THEN THE MIDFIELDER PASSES IT BACK TO THE WING WHO USUALLY HAS A SHOT ON GOAL.

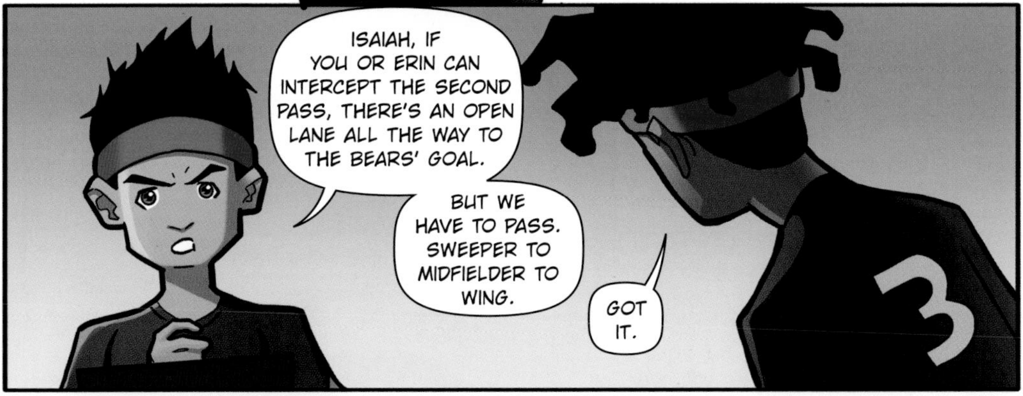
ISAIAH, IF YOU OR ERIN CAN INTERCEPT THE SECOND PASS, THERE'S AN OPEN LANE ALL THE WAY TO THE BEARS' GOAL.
BUT WE HAVE TO PASS. SWEEPER TO MIDFIELDER TO WING.
GOT IT.

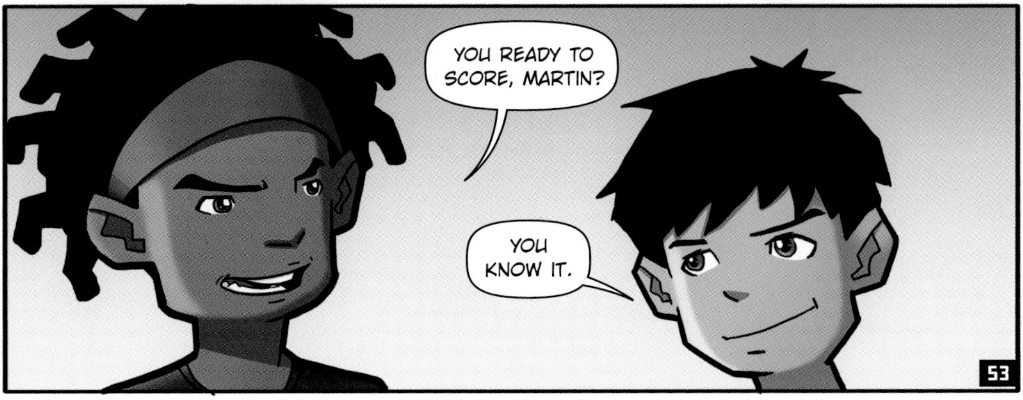
YOU READY TO SCORE, MARTIN?
YOU KNOW IT.

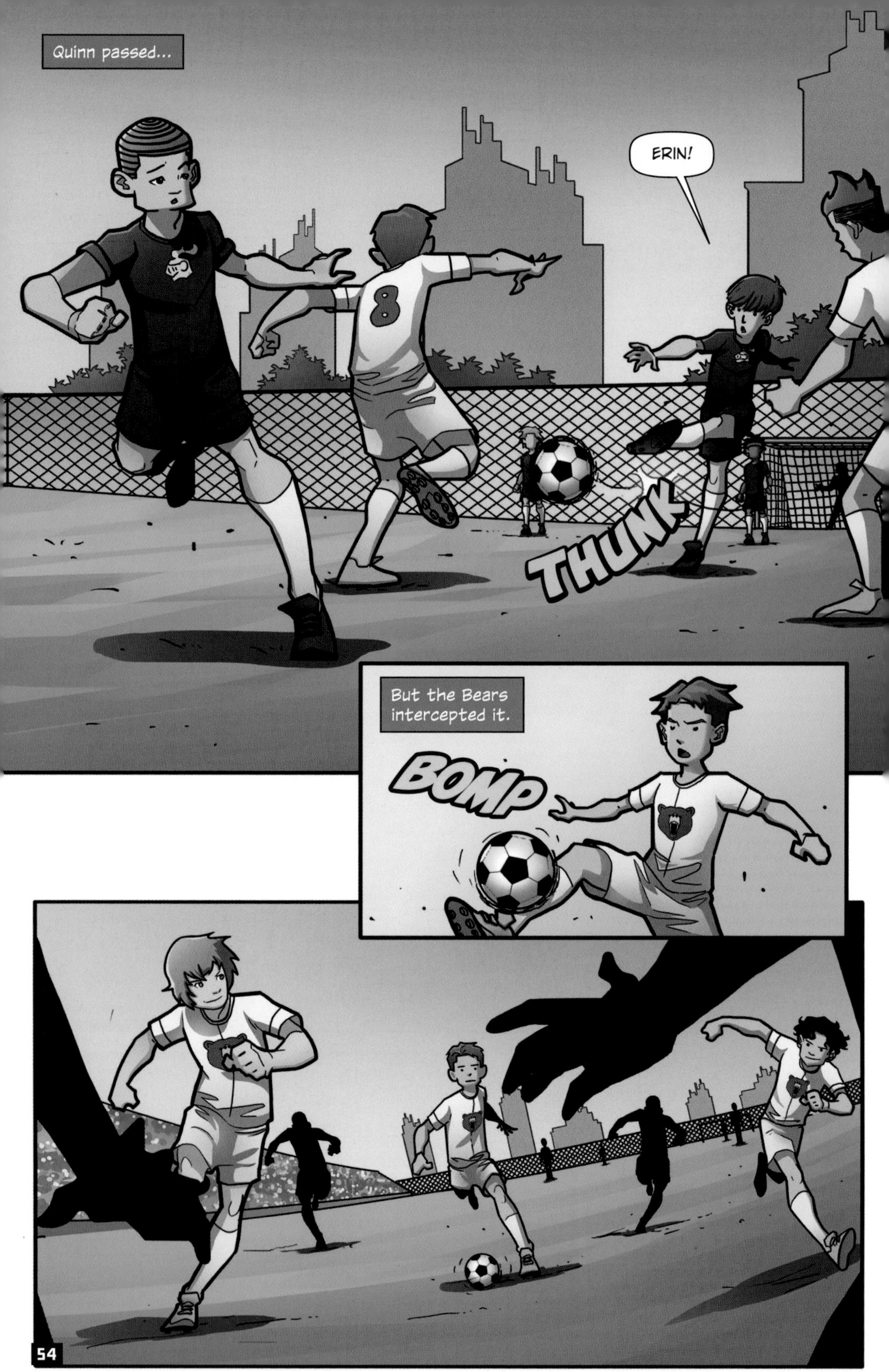

Quinn passed...
ERIN!
THUNK
But the Bears intercepted it.
BOMP

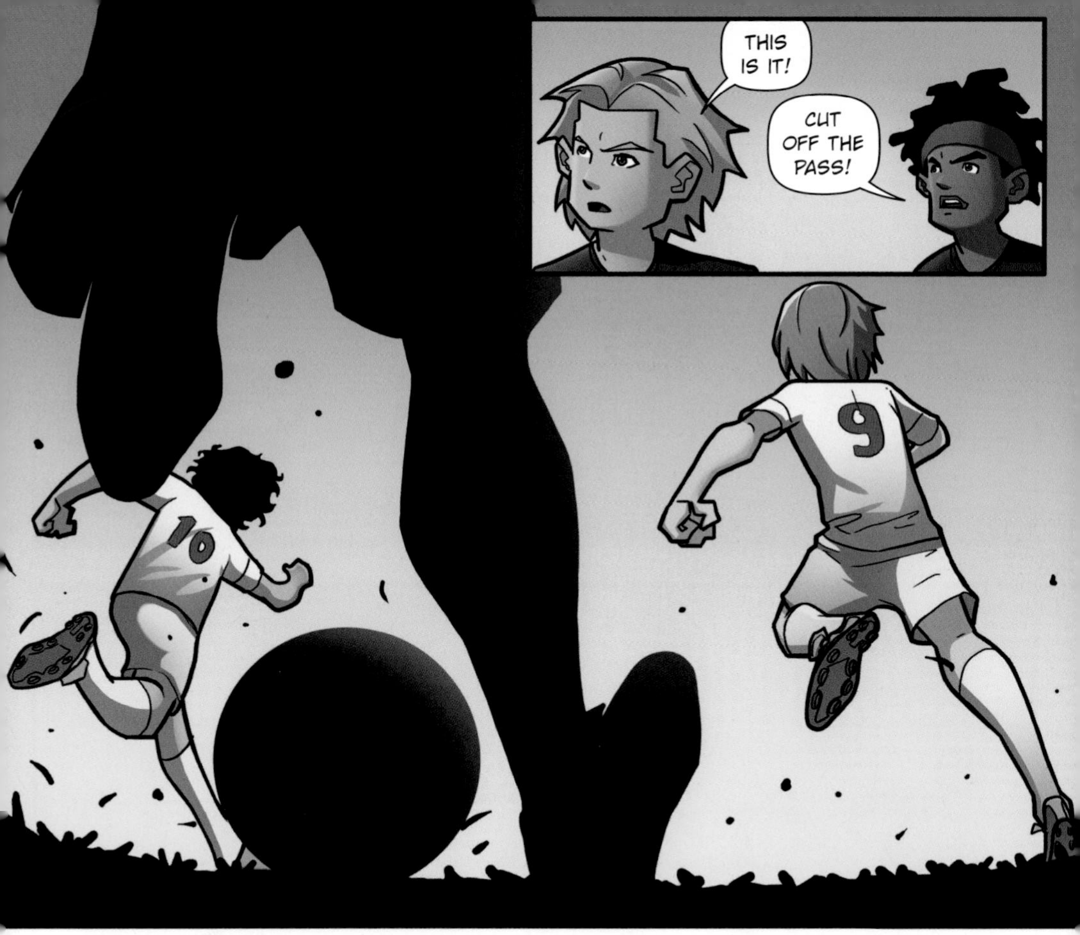
THIS IS IT!
CUT OFF THE PASS!

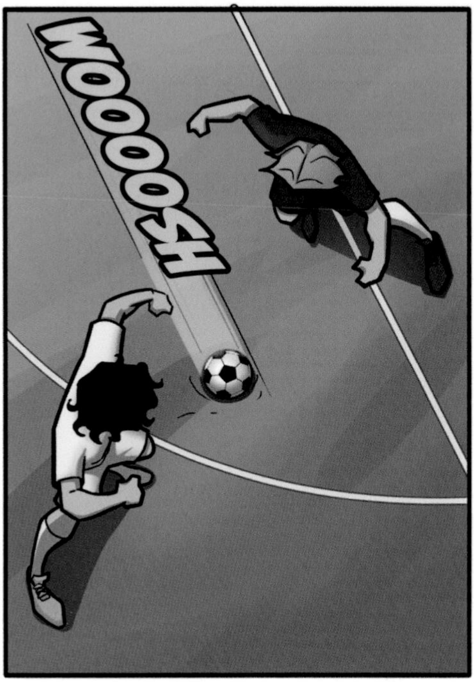
WOOOOOSH

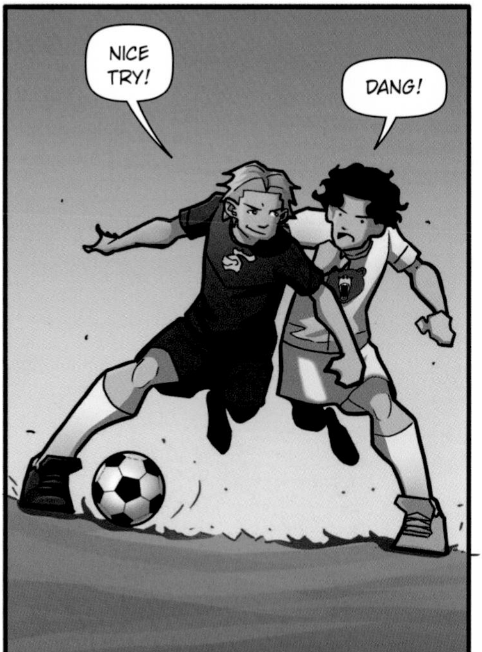
NICE TRY!
DANG!

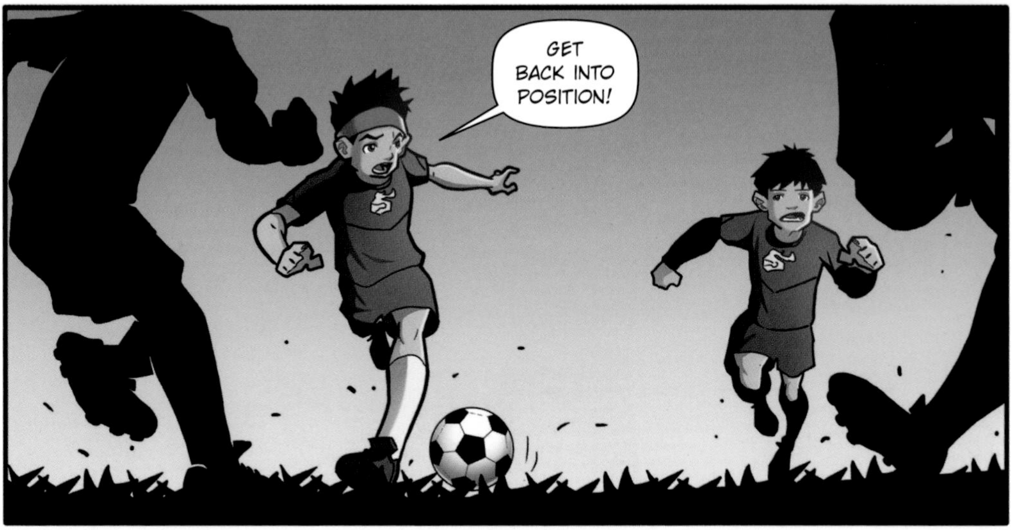
GET BACK INTO POSITION!

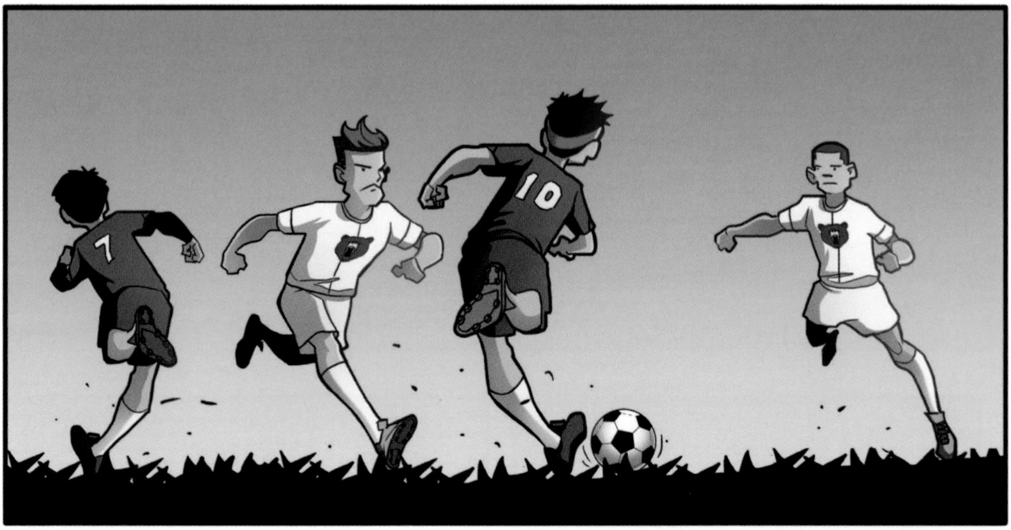
7
10

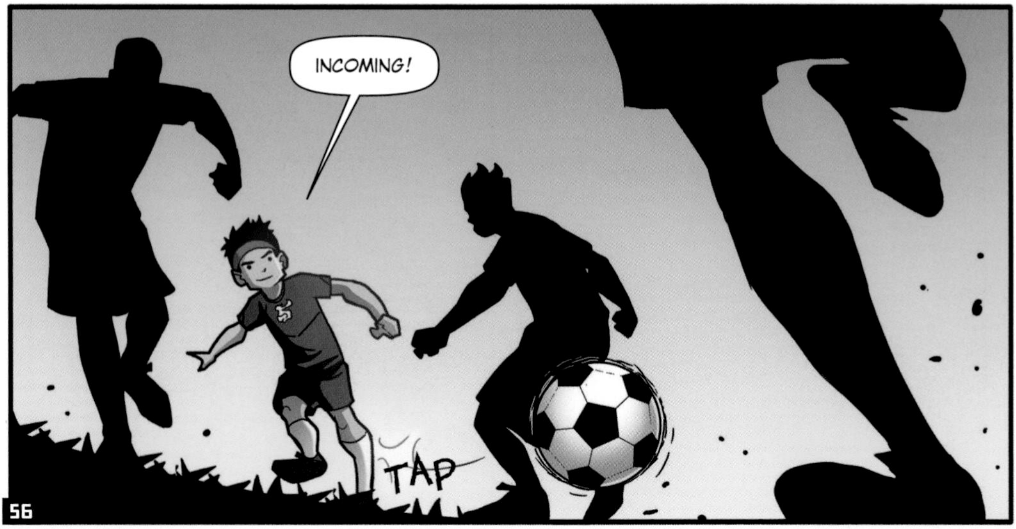
INCOMING!
TAP

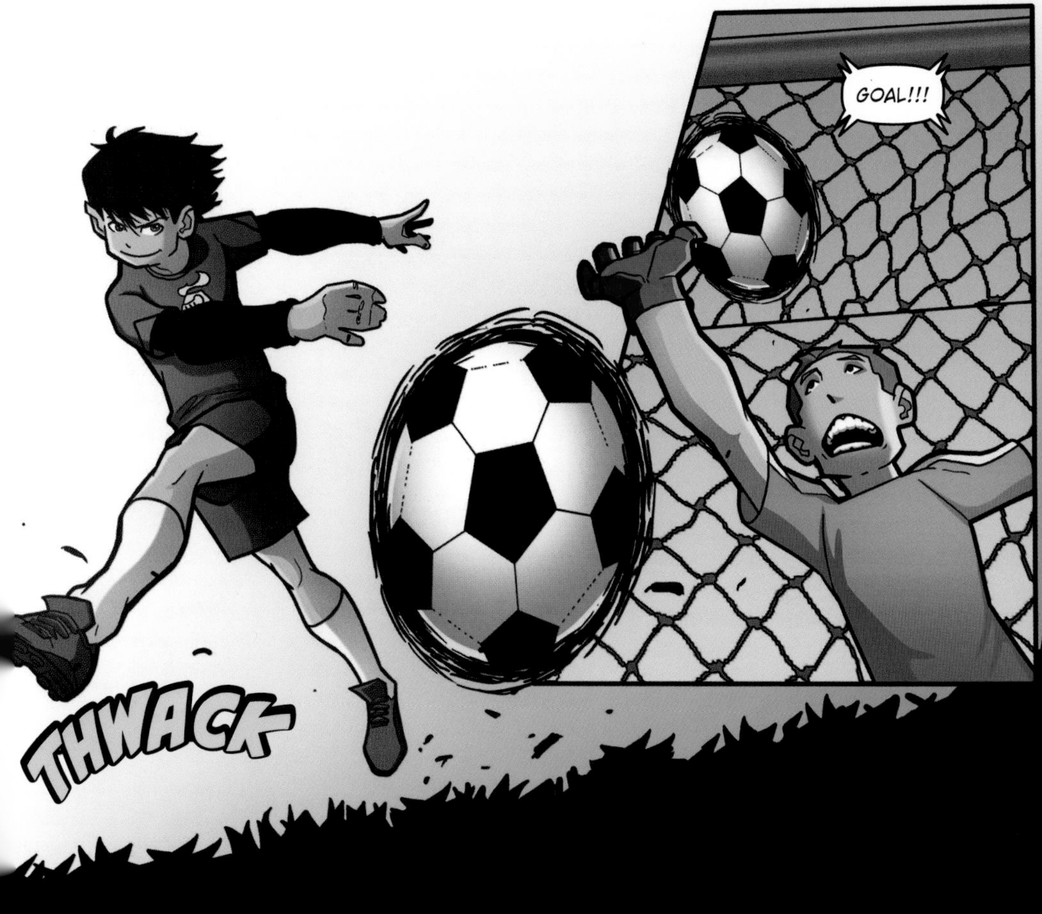
GOAL!!!
THWACK

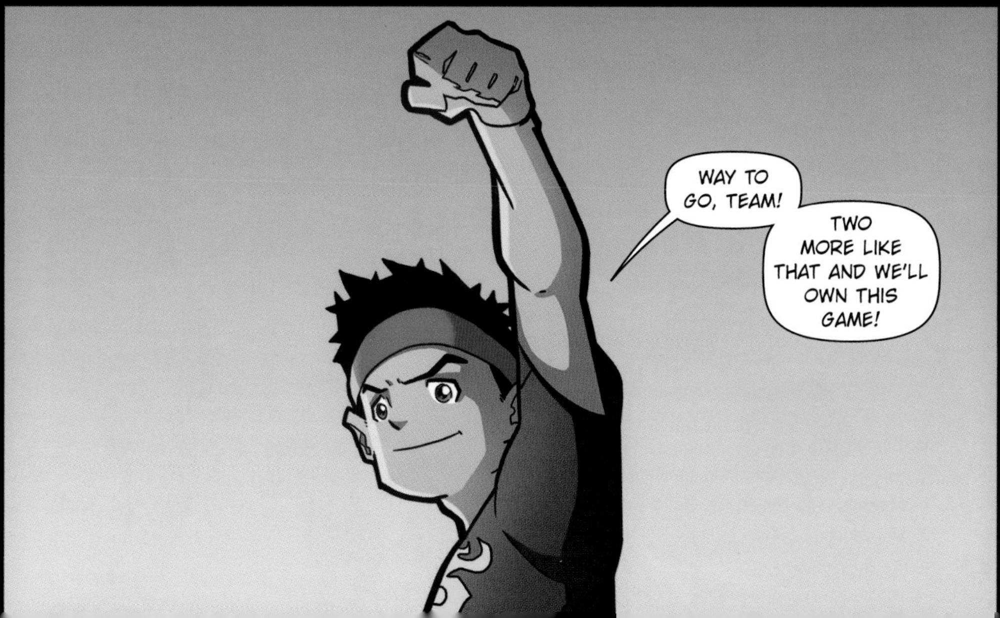
WAY TO GO, TEAM!
TWO MORE LIKE THAT AND WE'LL OWN THIS GAME!

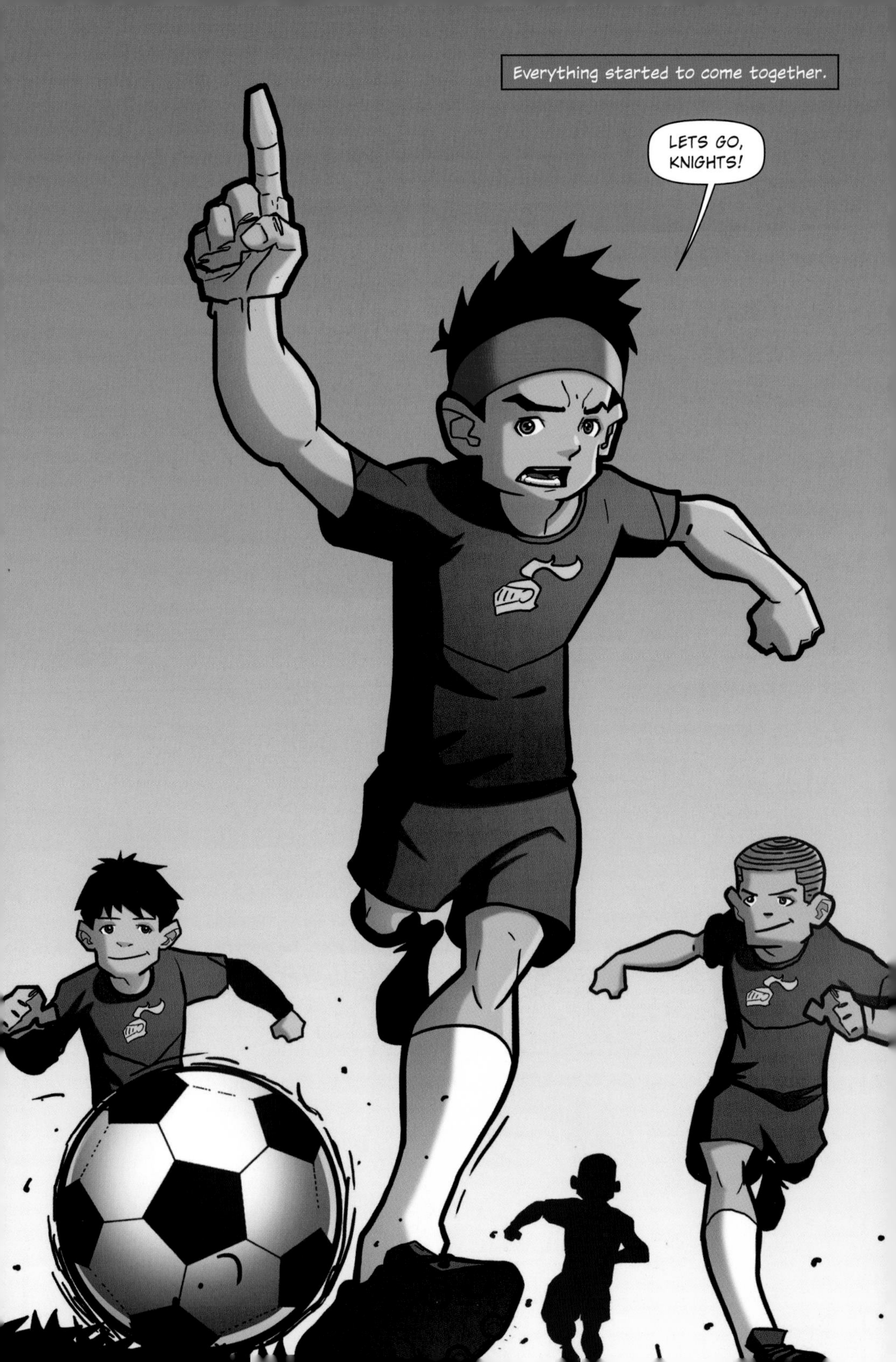
Everything started to come together.
LETS GO, KNIGHTS!

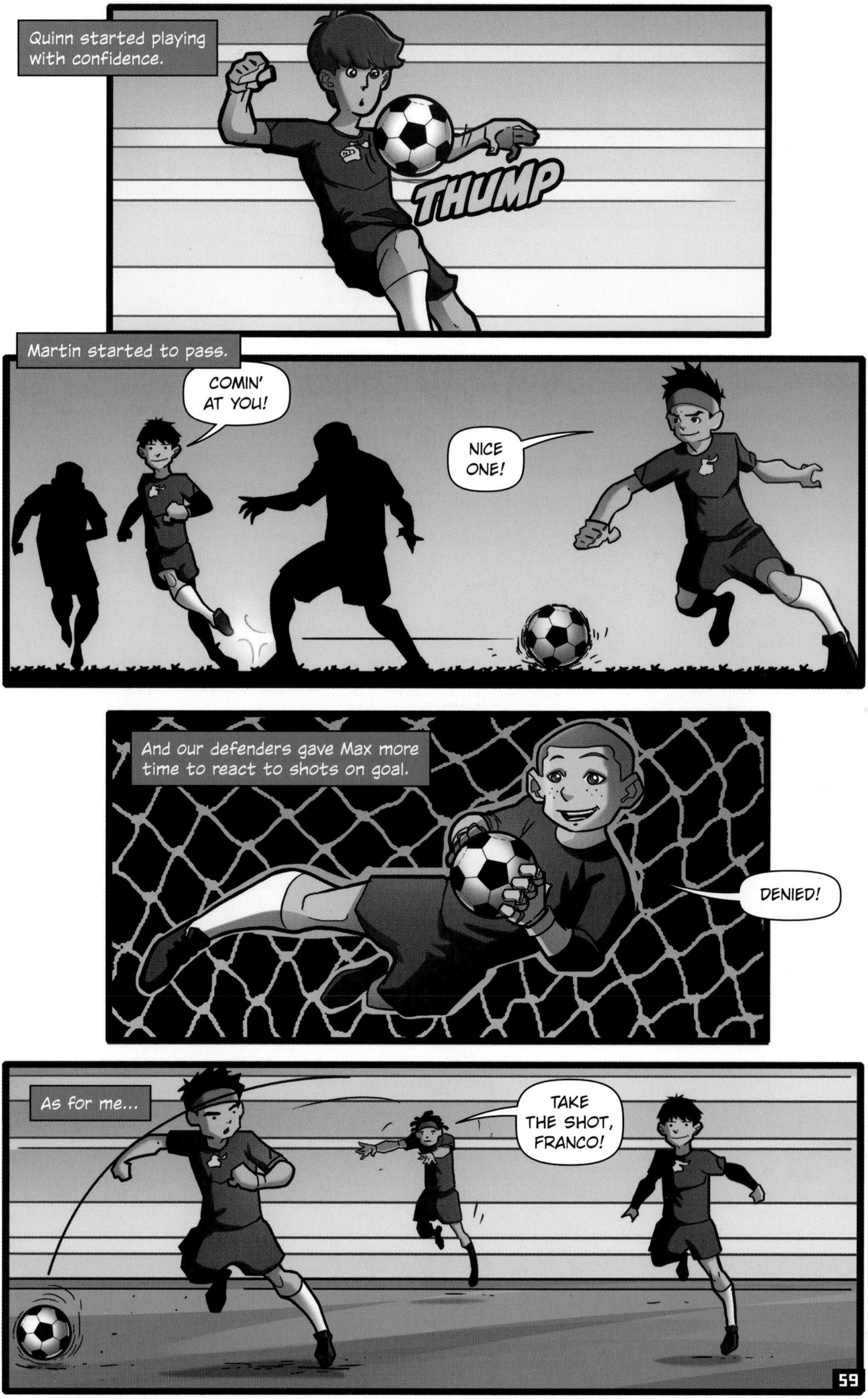

Quinn started playing with confidence.
THUMP
Martin started to pass.
COMIN' AT YOU!
NICE ONE!
And our defenders gave Max more time to react to shots on goal.
DENIED!
As for me...
TAKE THE SHOT, FRANCO!

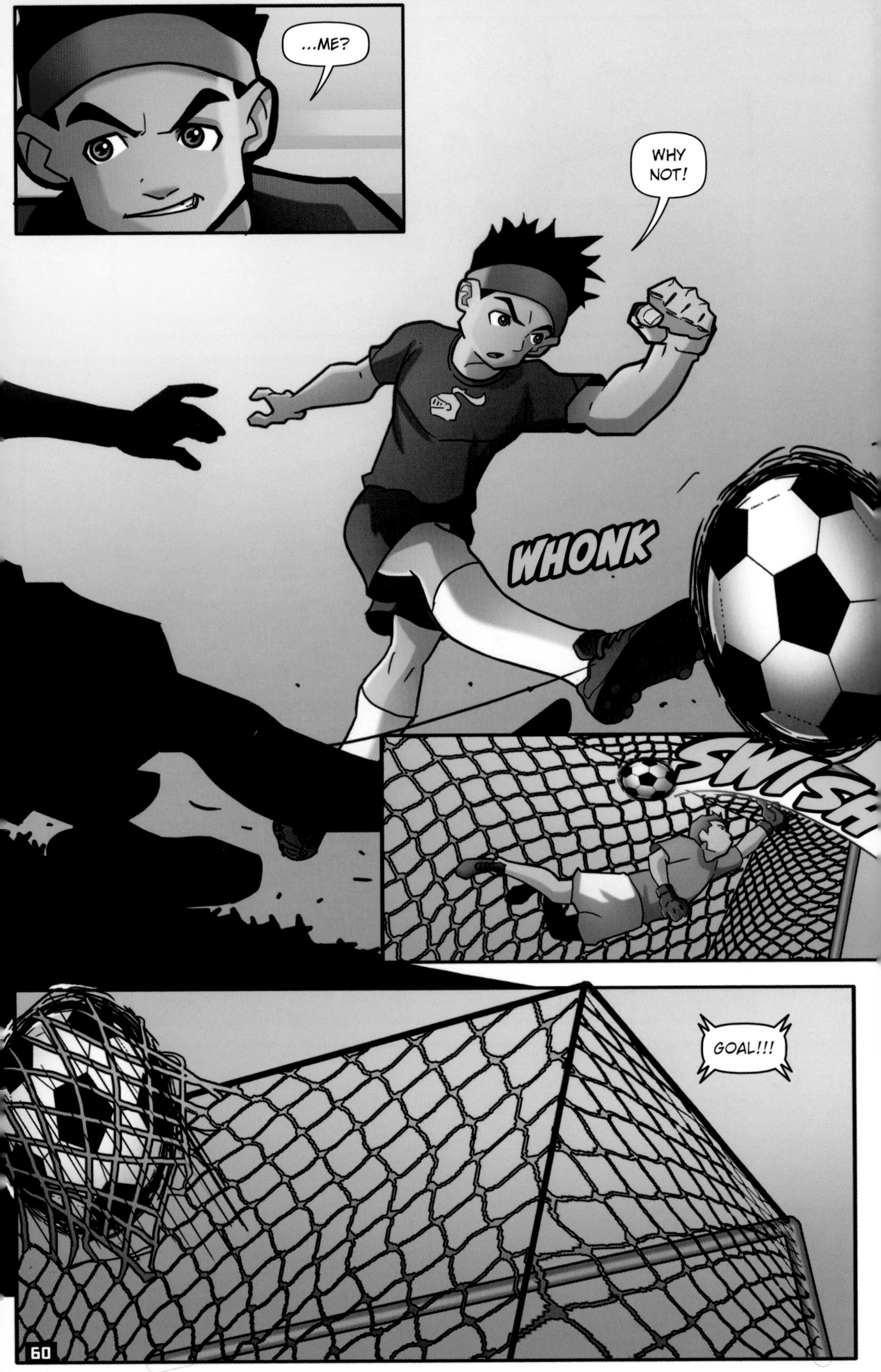
...ME?
WHY NOT!
WHONK
SWISH
GOAL!!!

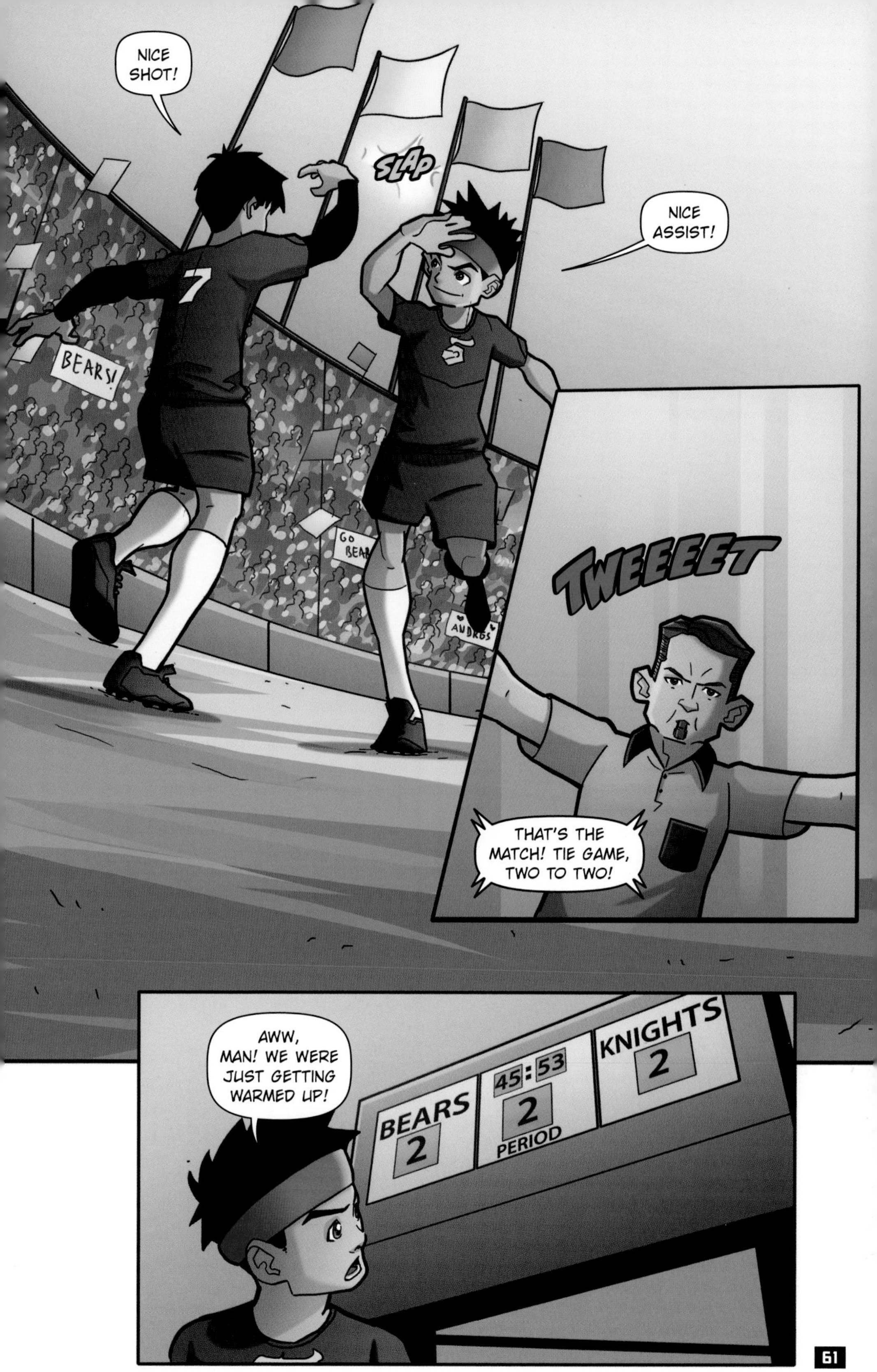
NICE SHOT!
SLAP
NICE ASSIST!
BEARS!
GO BEARS
TWEEEET
THAT'S THE MATCH! TIE GAME, TWO TO TWO!
AWW, MAN! WE WERE JUST GETTING WARMED UP!
BEARS 2
45:53 2 PERIOD
KNIGHTS 2

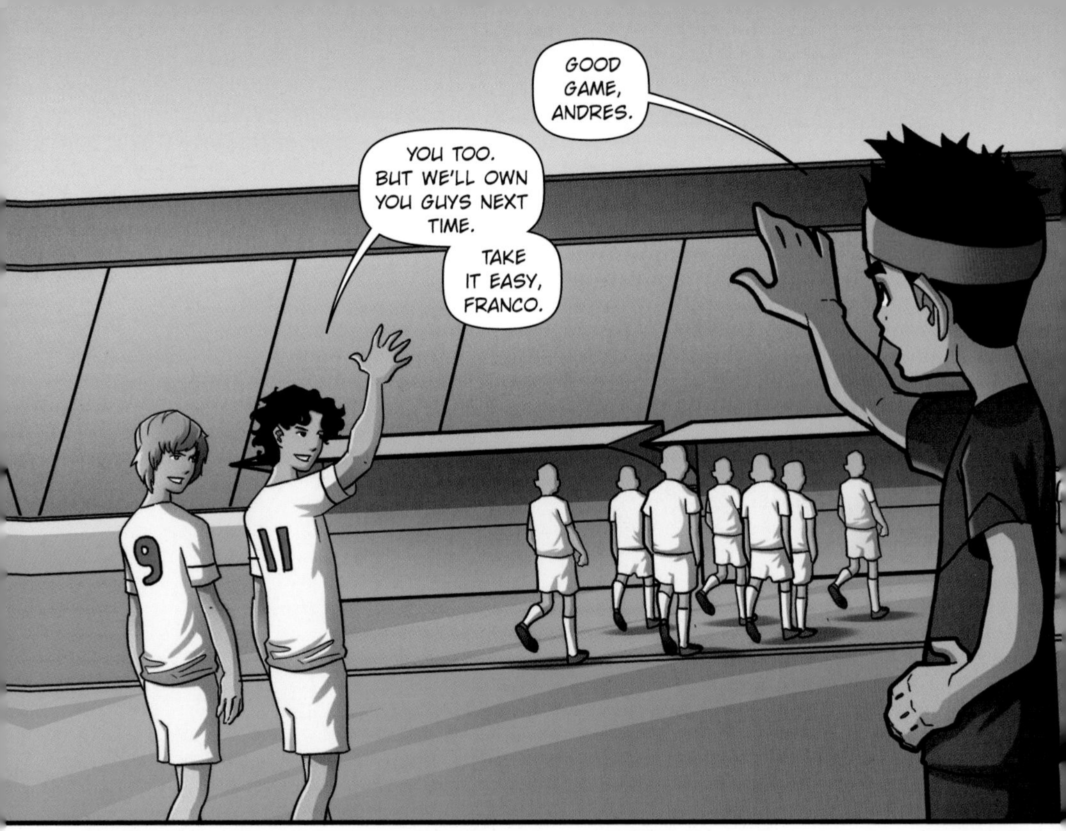
GOOD GAME, ANDRES.
YOU TOO. BUT WE'LL OWN YOU GUYS NEXT TIME.
TAKE IT EASY, FRANCO.

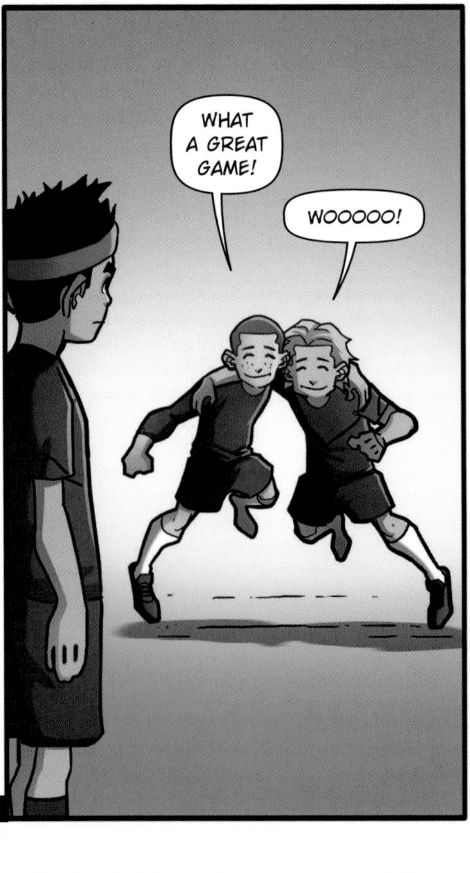
WHAT A GREAT GAME!
WOOOOO!

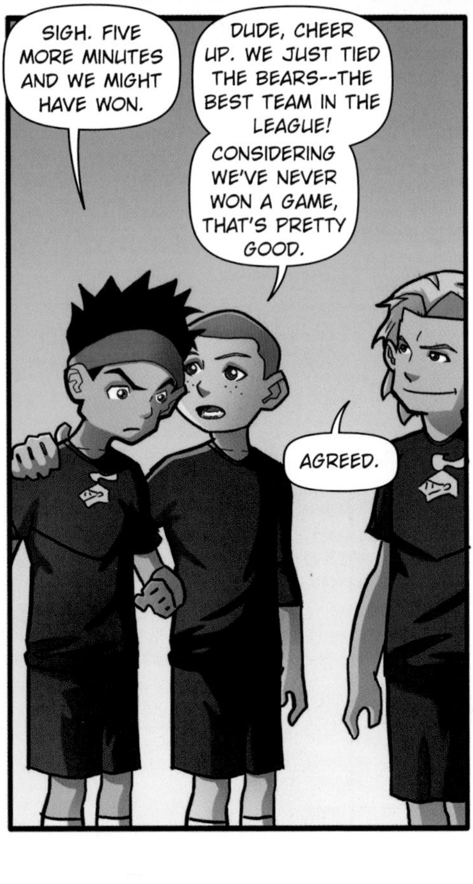
SIGH. FIVE MORE MINUTES AND WE MIGHT HAVE WON.
DUDE, CHEER UP. WE JUST TIED THE BEARS--THE BEST TEAM IN THE LEAGUE!
CONSIDERING WE'VE NEVER WON A GAME, THAT'S PRETTY GOOD.
AGREED.

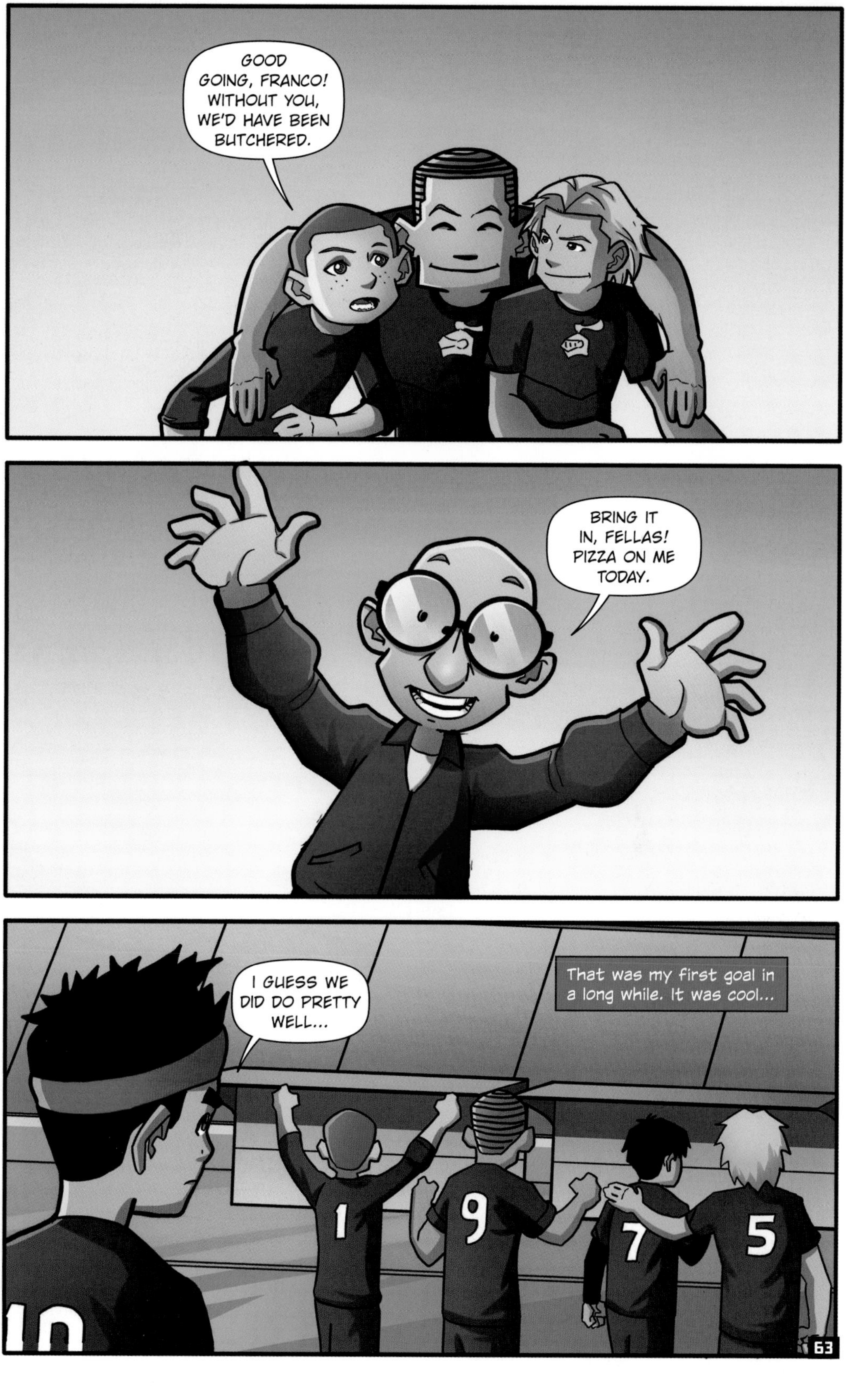
GOOD GOING, FRANCO! WITHOUT YOU, WE'D HAVE BEEN BUTCHERED.
BRING IT IN, FELLAS! PIZZA ON ME TODAY.
I GUESS WE DID DO PRETTY WELL...
That was my first goal in a long while. It was cool...
10
1
9
7
5

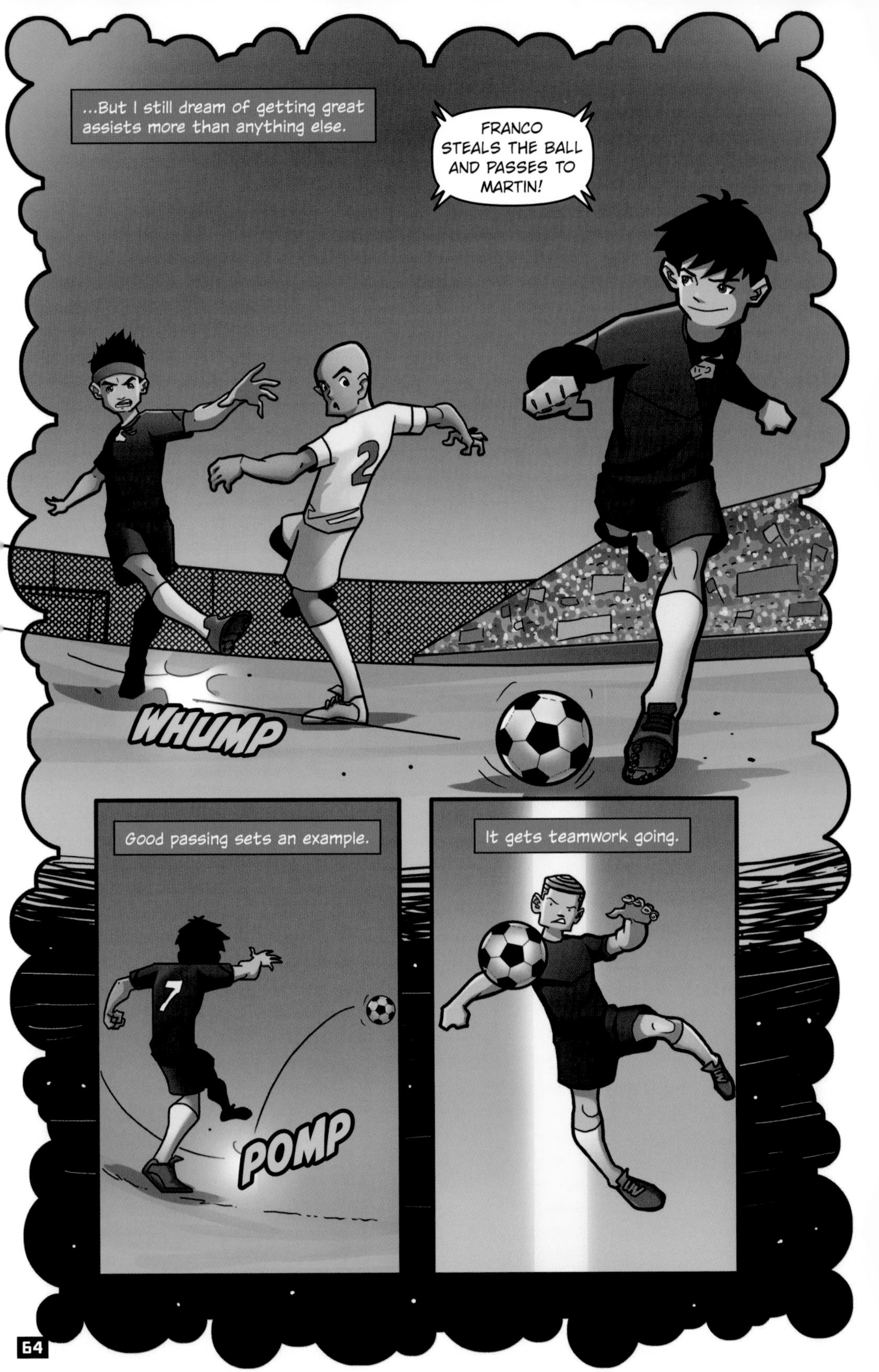
...But I still dream of getting great assists more than anything else.
FRANCO STEALS THE BALL AND PASSES TO MARTIN!
WHUMP
Good passing sets an example.
7
POMP
It gets teamwork going.

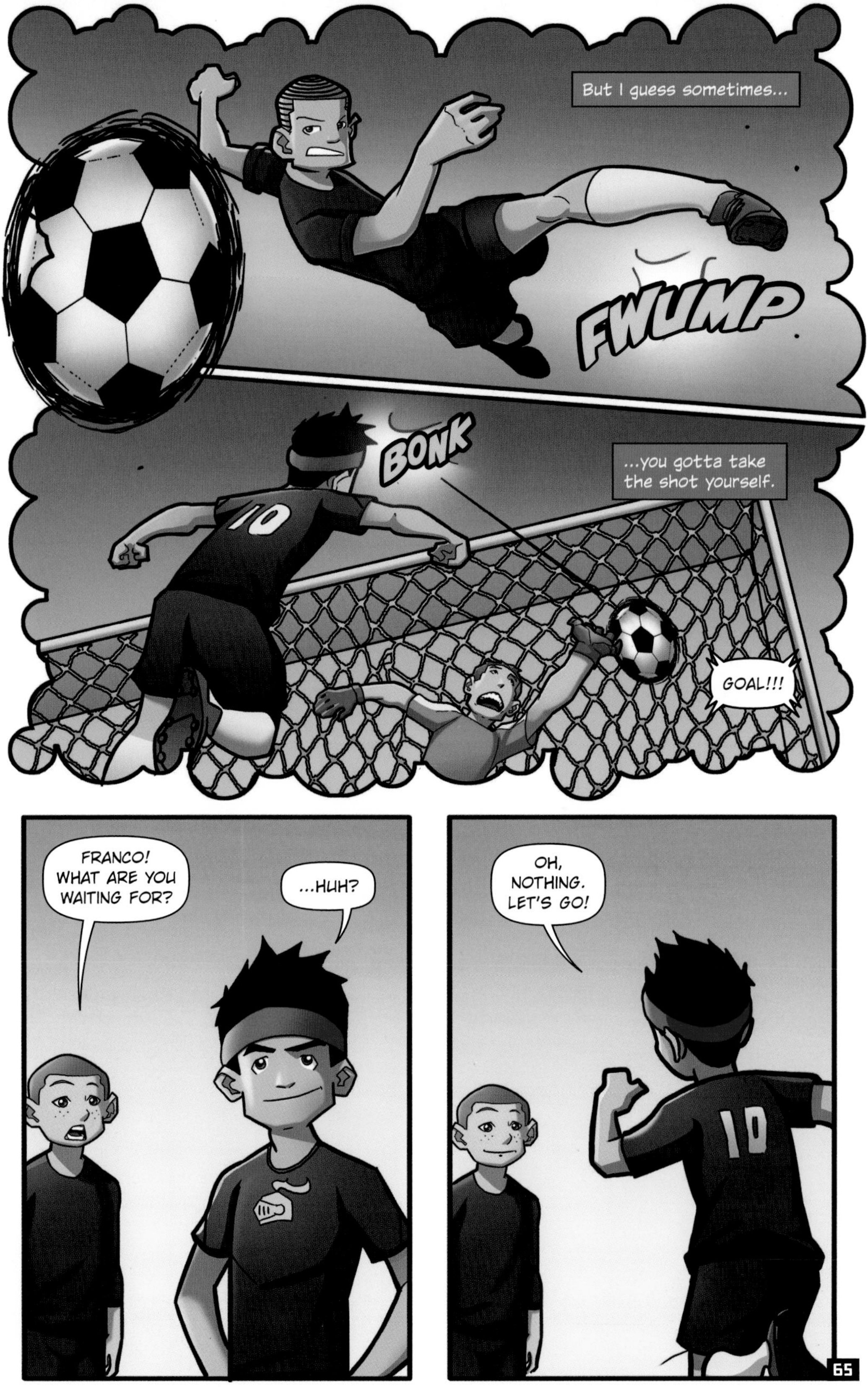
But I guess sometimes...
FWUMP
BONK
...you gotta take the shot yourself.
GOAL!!!
FRANCO! WHAT ARE YOU WAITING FOR?
...HUH?
OH, NOTHING. LET'S GO!
10

ABOUT THE AUTHOR

RICARDO SANCHEZ is a writer, Emmy-winning creator, and executive producer. His comic book credits include Batman: Legends of the Dark Knight, Resident Evil, RIFT: Telara Chronicles, and many others. When he's not writing comics, Ricardo maintains a vintage toy blog, drives 70's muscle cars, and shops year-round for Halloween decorations for his home in Redwood City, California.

ABOUT THE ILLUSTRATOR

Based in Malaysia, artist **IAN WARYANTO**'s work has appeared in several independent comics, including Monster Ninjas.

ABOUT THE LETTERER

JAYMES REED has operated the company Digital-CAPS: Comic Book Lettering since 2003. He has done lettering for many publishers, most notably and recently Avatar Press. He's also the only letterer working with Inception Strategies, an Aboriginal-Australian publisher that develops social comics with public service messages for the Australian government. Jaymes also a 2012 & 2013 Shel Dorf Award Nominee.

GLOSSARY

ASSIST (uh-SISST)—if you got an assist in soccer, you passed to a teammate who scored shortly after receiving the pass

CLOBBER (KLOB-er)—defeat decisively

INTERCEPT (in-ter-SEPT)—to stop something by getting in the way of it

LURE (LOO-er)—to draw something or someone closer, as in bait used to catch fish while fishing

MASTERFUL (MASS-ter-full)—if you are masterful, you show great skill at doing something particular

MIDFIELDER (MID-feel-der)—a player active in the midfield of soccer who plays a role on offense and defense

PRACTICALLY (PRAK-tik-lee)—almost, nearly, or virtually

RECRUITED (ri-KROO-tid)—enlisted, drafted, or accepted into a group or organization

SCOUT (SKOUT)—a person sent out to obtain information

SWEEPER (SWEE-per)—a player who supports the main defenders, often by intercepting the ball

ZONE (ZOHN)—in soccer, a player's zone is the area of the field they are responsible for

VISUAL QUESTIONS

1. The soccer ball in this panel is warped. Why did the illustrator decide to do this? How does it change the way the panel feels?

2. In this panel, tiny stars are floating around Franco's head. What do they mean? How does Franco feel here?

3. Franco has to beat the odds in this book. In what ways does Franco help his teammates? Find as many examples as you can.

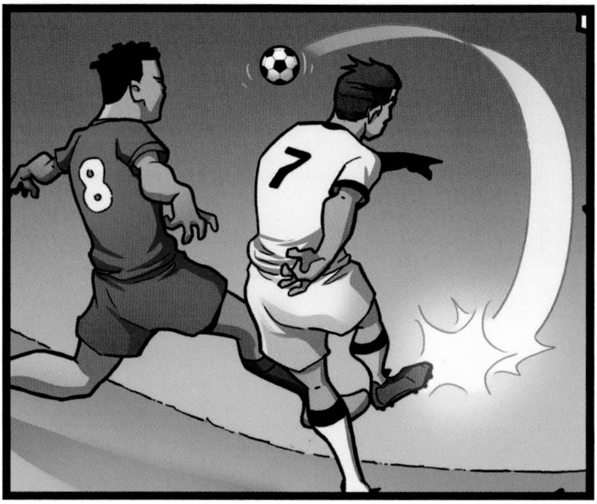

4. We see the path of travel for the soccer ball in this panel. What other ways might the illustrator be able to show the path the ball travels?

5. The soccer ball passes over the panel border here. Why do you think the comic book's creators decided to do this? How does it affect the way the panel feels and looks to you?

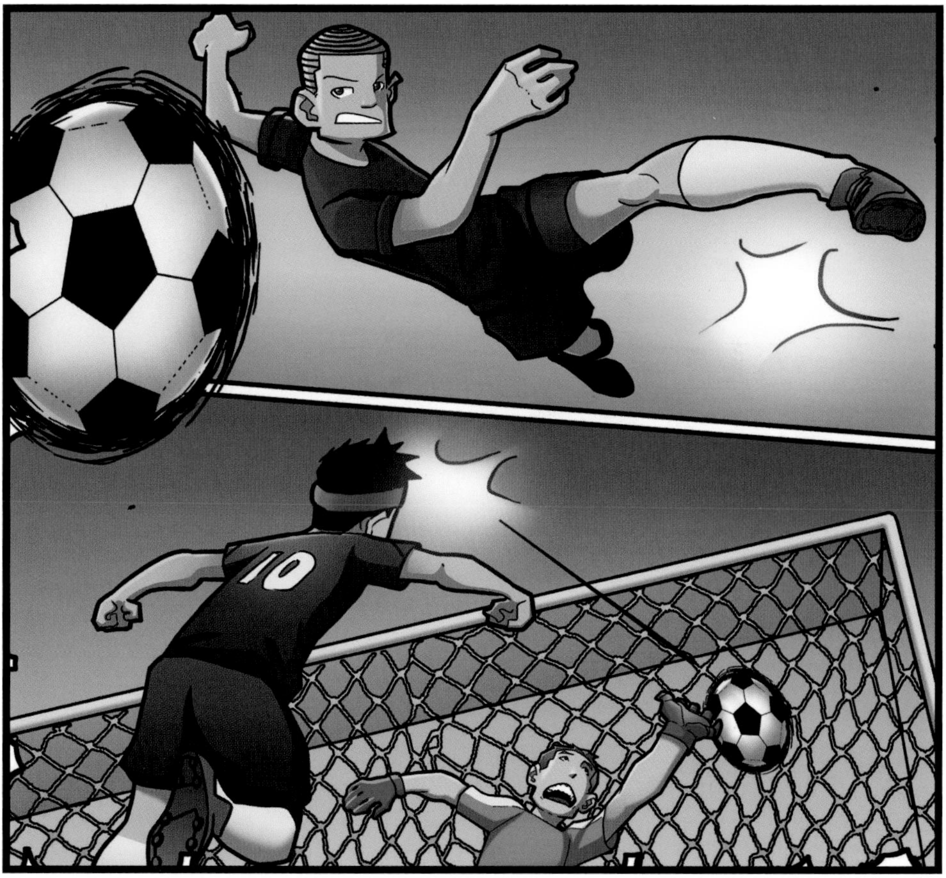

AD THEM ALL!

Sports Illustrated KIDS
GRAPHIC NOVELS
8-BIT
BASEBALL
TERRELL · FERRARA

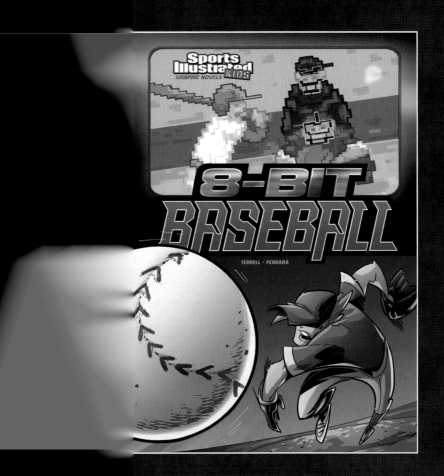

SEBALL

s undefeated in baseball games--video games, anyway. But when he best friend, Jared is forced to get off the couch and step onto the ol's baseball team tryouts. Despite the fact that he's never even held e, Jared ends up being pretty impressive as a pitcher--until the line ames and reality begins to blur. Can Jared sort out the glitch in his

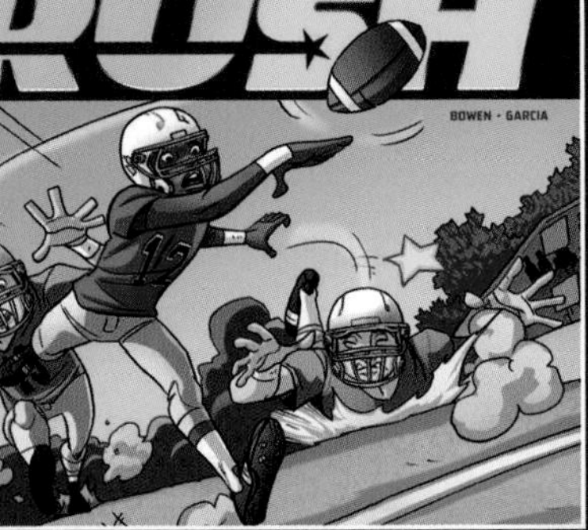
BOWEN · GARCIA

of getting hit. With a little help from his teammates, Steve goes to great lengths to toughen up Aaron only to discover that toughness isn't the quarterback's actual problem.

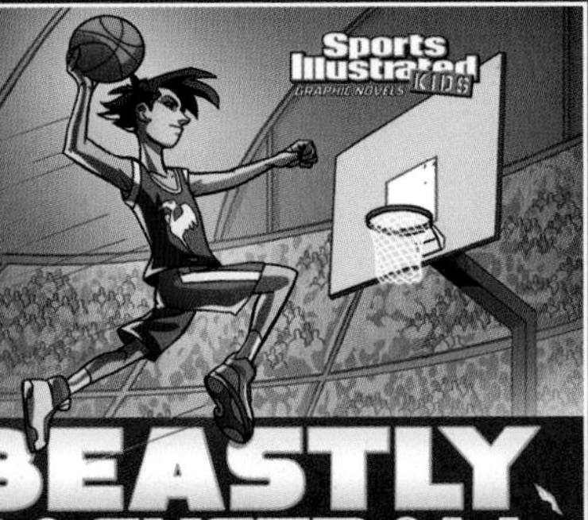
Sports Illustrated KIDS
GRAPHIC NOVELS

BEASTLY BASKETBAL

Joe knows kung fu. In fact, he loves it mo than anything. Every single evening, Joe walks to his neighborhood kung fu studio to practice for hours on end . . . until the day he arrives to find his studio is closed. So Joe decides to pursue his second-favorite activity—basketball. He joins his

KNIGHTS
SOCCER

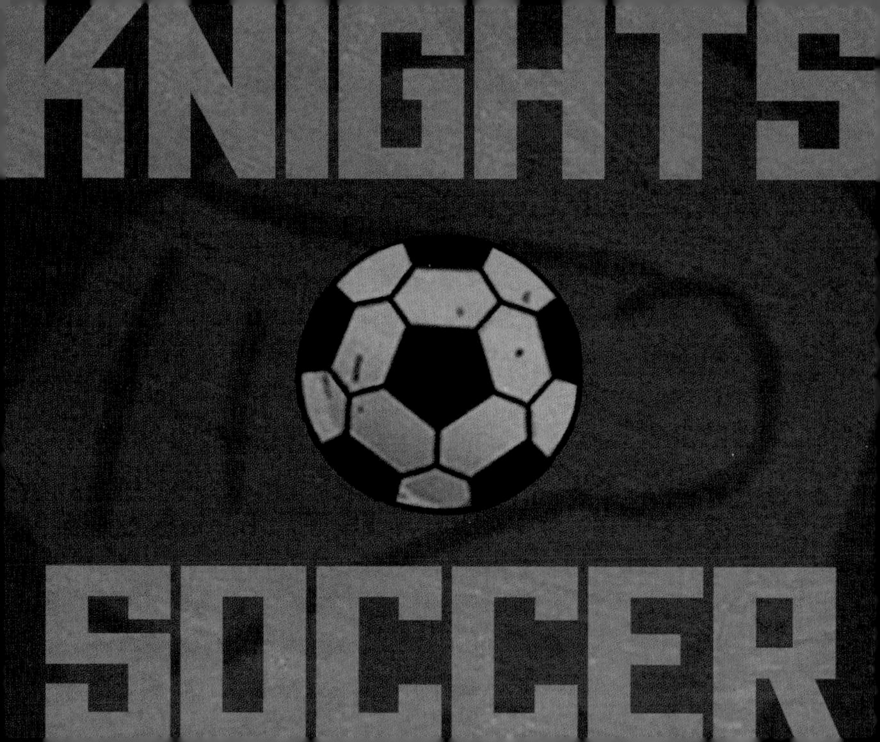